NYGHT LYGHT PUBLISHING LLC

Tales From The Night

My Haunted Summer

Being my first publication, I would like to dedicate this to my dad. Life isn't the same without you. You are, and will always be, greatly missed.

S. E. Shelton

Special Thanks:

I would like to thank my wife for assisting with the editing process, as well as encouraging me to write.

I also want to thank family, friends, and co-workers for encouraging me.

Last, but most importantly, I want to thank God for giving me a desire to write.

Another school year slowly came to an end. I had been anxiously awaiting summer all school year, well, ever since fall break anyway. During fall break my big brother took me on a stroll through the woods. It was amazing to say the least, as we had discovered several memorable places. Probably one of my personal favorites was a huge cliff deep in the woods.

A solid rock wall stood high enough to scrape the clouds, or it appeared that tall from our vantage point. I know what you are thinking, if you have seen one rock wall you have saw them all. Not true in this case. A distinctive feature about this particular wall was near the top of it, and an improvised way to get there.

Located about mid-way, we found a section that was indented, like a sharp V-shape in the rock structure. Placed sturdily in the indented area, was a very resourceful man-made ladder. I had seen areas similar to this on television shows, and movies all about surviving in the wild, and having only the bare essentials in some of the worst-case scenarios. Simply looking at the ladder, I could easily picture someone wielding an ax, hatchet, or machete to hack down small trees to construct the ladder. Each rung on it was secured in place with small vines wrapped and tied tightly around every last one. The ladder only went up around three fourths of the wall, and at the top was a small oval shaped opening.

Me? I was simply in awe at the sight, not sure what to think or even expect for that matter. My mind automatically went into horror film come true mode, thinking a monster or cannibal would be lurking in the oval shaped opening atop the ladder, or on its way back for the night after capturing a tasty meal…. hopefully not us!!

However, my big brother, Joe, is fearless and slightly more adventurous than I have always been. He scurried up the ladder for a closer inspection, while I was still planted firmly on the ground. My heart raced, fearing for his life as well as my own. Who knew what he would find in there, or what would find me before he got back down? Luckily, there was nothing there.

"I like that!" Joe said excitedly. "I bet someone made this ladder, and even chiseled out this area to use as a deer stand! I just love this whole idea! It is living off the land at its finest!"

"It is pretty cool. Definitely not something you see every day." I replied trying not to sound completely terrified.

Another area we found that sent my mind wandering and thinking about old Vietnam movies, was located in a hollow near a waterfall. The hills were steep, sprouting apart and veering away from each other a broad distance until halting to form the water fall. A small creek twisted and turned going this way then that, all the way to the end. Several tall trees had fallen in that area at the bottom of the hills. We used some of them to cross the creek in various areas when our path was blocked, and maybe a couple of times just because it was fun.

The old war movie look was contributed to a combination of lively green vines, weeds, and moss… lots and lots of moss covering everything. So much moss it would almost make one despise it. It blanketed the majority of the area. The tall fallen trees were totally engulfed by moss. A thin layer of steam from the cool creek water plummeting into the warm lake, lurked in the area as well. Everything combined, gave it one eerie feel. Making a great setting for a scene of soldiers facing an ambush, while fighter jets zoomed in to blast away at the evil opposing army, easily imaginable.

Nearing the waterfall itself, I stopped short, way short of the very edge. Joe, being fearless, walked all the way to the very edge to look over. I most certainly was not that brave. I'm terrified of heights. That is the main reason I stayed off of the ladder earlier. From where I stood, it looked as though we were smack dab in the middle of a creepy picture someone had flawlessly painted. Where the hills stopped, there was nothing beyond that point other than the white and blue of the sky. To me, it actually appeared as though the land, the entire world itself, had been sliced apart. I know the earth is round, but the image before me really had me thinking it was flat, and we had just discovered one edge of the world. I almost wish I had walked up to the edge to look over. I'm sure the view would have been breath taking. My fear of heights knows no limits, which can be a bummer sometimes.

"Hello!! Earth to Shawn. Can you hear me?!!??" Mr. Doyle yelled.

"Yeah. Sorry. What?" I replied quickly.

"It is your turn to read aloud. Have you been following along? Do you even know where we are at?" He Said angrily as some of the other students snickered and laughed.

"Of course, we are at school." I replied as the giggle bug hit me as well. Before he could threaten me with time-out or the principal, the bell came to my rescue.

Mr. Doyle had black hair that he always parted to the left side. He wore small square black framed glasses, that sheltered his piercing blue eyes. As I got up to exit class with the rest of the students, I could almost see his long hair puffing up and down. The steam from his exploding temper, seemed like smoke signals. I diverted my gaze and hurried out before he could say anything further.

"That was a good one man, were you asleep or day dreaming though?" Mike asked, when I got to my locker, which was located right beside of his. Mike was about the same height as me, but stocky. Most of the time, when people use the term stocky, they use it as a polite way to say that a person is chubby. Such is the case with myself. I'm often referred to as stocky, but I am far from being in denial. I am absolutely chubby, hovering on the border of fat. The difference between Mike and I being, Mike is solid. When he falls down in the gym, it sounds like a boulder crashing on the floor. Me? I'm the kid that makes the ugly splat sound, followed up with some embarrassing jiggling action from all parts of my body.

"I was just day dreaming. I hate when we have to read aloud. It always makes me drowsy." I replied with a smile.

"Well, you need to stay awake around him. I think Mr. Doyle just stays in a bad mood for some reason. The least little thing sets him off, and he gets really mad, really fast." Mike said seriously.

"Yeah, I know. He kind of scares me a little. I'm just glad this is the last day of school." I replied happily.

"Hey guys, I know why he's in such a bad mood today!" Kenneth exclaimed. Kenneth is the athletic type. I can imagine him being born holding a basketball, and crying when the doctor took it away. He's always on the move, basketball, baseball, track, if it is a sport, he plays it. He is actually good at these sports. His super thick, super big glasses are misleading. You see those and doubt he could even see a backboard if he were standing right under it.

"why?" Mike and I asked eagerly.

"You know how Jon is always picking on Eric?" Kenneth asked sadly.

"Yes. He needs to be put in his place." Mike answered sounding upset.

"What happened already?" I asked impatiently. The clock was ticking, and my next class was PE. To make matters worse, the gym is on the opposite side of the school. Not to mention, down stairs from where we currently were.

"Both of them are in his second period, right? Ok, so this morning during their class, Mr. Doyle had to step out for whatever reason. Jon started smacking Eric in the back of the head really hard, and I do mean HARD. I guess Eric decided to stand up for himself. After it had gone on for about ten minutes. He stood up, turned around, and opened his mouth to say something." Kenneth rambled in a hurry.

"AND!!!????" -Mike and I chorused together.

"And then, Jon smacked him right in the face with his notebook." Kenneth said, as though it were a big deal.

"What??" I asked, not very impressed with the story.

"That's it? That was the big show down?" Mike said, failing to see why Kenneth was so excited about it.

"Yes. Mr. Doyle got back right after it happened, and had to send Eric to the nurse. The wire from the spine of the notebook was stuck in Eric's right eye." Kenneth replied, looking like he was about to vomit.

"Ouch. That hurts just hearing about it." Mike said, unconsciously rubbing his right eye.

"What about Jon? Did he get into trouble?" I asked curiously.

"None whatsoever. Just like every other time he has been busted for bullying someone. Mr. Doyle's face turned every color possible while looking at Jon. Finally, he gave Jon a warning. He told him he did not care if his dad was the Principal or not, the next time it happened, he would be in big trouble, and to mark his words. Then Jon just laughed and asked him 'Really? Go ahead and try to do something now. We both know you can't!" Kenneth's report of the events, were truly sickening.

"That makes me sick. Jon was held back two years to play basketball. I guess that would make sense if he were actually any good at it, but he is terrible. He has to be the oldest sixth grader in history, and I heard he is going to stay behind again next year." Mike said jokingly.

"I hope he does. Good riddance if you ask me. Not much of a serious threat though, Mr. Doyle's on the last day of school. Maybe he knows Jon is going to stay back and is letting him know he won't tolerate it another year." I said, trying to find logic in it all.

"Crap, that's the tardy bell, and I've got to run down stairs!! I've got Home Economics!" Kenneth blurted, becoming a blur and disappearing down the hall.

Jon, bully extraordinaire. I had my own issues with him back in fourth grade. Every day my fourth-grade year was pure torture. I never had the wire from a notebook spine stuck in my eye, but getting smacked in the head, wet willies, poked, kicked, punched….it really was a long list. All day, every day, and all school year long basically. At first, I got mad and demanded he quit, unfortunately for me, things just got worse. I asked the teacher to rethink our assigned seats, but she refused, and, as with all others, ignored the situation for fear of retaliation from Jon's dad. It got to the point where I absolutely hated going to school. My grades fell low enough the teacher recommended me for after school tutoring. I knew the content we were going over to a T, but no one seemed to care about the distractions I faced on a daily basis. At the end of the school year, my big brother had noticed bruises and inquired as to how I had gotten them. I told him everything hoping he would/could step in and help me out. To my dismay, he told me flat out that I needed to stand up to the bully, or he would kick my butt himself. I managed to keep things quiet the rest of the fourth-grade year. I was way more terrified of my brother than I was of Jon.

On the very first day of fifth grade, around second period, I heard some nerve rattling news. Evidently, during first period, Jon and his best, new, and only bud Bryce, decided it would be a good idea to pick on another guy in our grade, Mason. Mason was almost as tall as Jon, but he was super skinny and not as muscled up as the other two were. The words falling from everyone's lips was how the two caught Mason in the restroom, beat him so bad he was puking blood, and had to be taken to the hospital. I knew if that happened to me, I would not be able to hide that from my brother, and in return, I would get what he promised me the minute I got home. I decided, and hoped, I could just avoid the duo that had been dubbed "the wrecking crew". My plan of avoidance worked pretty well, until I ran into them just before fourth period one day.

I figured between classes would be the best opportunity to use the restroom, considering all of the teachers seemed to frown upon those breaks occurring during class. I knew the rumor going around said they beat Mason to a pulp in the restroom, so needless to say, time was of the essence. I hurried and used the rest room as quickly as I could. Then raced out of the stall to wash my hands, and dry them. As the paper towels fell from my hand into the waste basket, so did my game plan, and my hope.

Distinctive laughter stabbed my ears as the duo waltzed into the restroom. Both of them paused just inside the door, Bryce looking at me wildly continuing to laugh, Jon looking at me with hate in his eyes. Seeing me there, his laughter stopping suddenly. I froze for a moment. I just knew I was done for. This was it; this was going to be my first-class ticket straight to the hospital. If Mason was puking blood according to the rumors, what about me? The same? Some broken bones? Would I even live long enough to make it to the hospital? I could tell from the looks in their eyes, and the drool oozing from their smiles, that they were starved for more mayhem.

I swiftly grabbed my books from the sink and darted toward the door. Jon and Bryce stepped closer together blocking my exit, I side stepped to go around, but they stepped farther apart with arms out stretched.

"Where do you think you are going?" Bryce barked, still laughing psychotically.

"What is your hurry? You should stay awhile porky!!" Jon said menacingly.

Without thinking, I clenched my fist and swung as hard as I could. Time stood still. My heart stopped. For a split second, long enough for me to think 'Oh God what am I doing? There are two of them and both are at least a foot taller than I am, and they look a lot stronger!!' Then…BAAAAMMM!!! Impact right on the tip of Jon's long, pointy nose. 'Crap, I'm dead now.' I thought. Bryce just laughed harder and louder than before as he staggered over and leaned on the wall for support. Bryce was holding his stomach, and pointing at Jon with hysteric laughter overcoming him. My eyes were still locked on Jon, as he grasped his bloody nose with both hands, tears rolling down both of his cheeks.

"What the heck was that for?" Jon begged.

"That's for every single day last year!!! Leave me alone this year, or you will get all of that you want and more!!" I grunted angrily, and glanced at Bryce. "You want some? I've got plenty to go around, and I will not be an easy target like Mason!!"

"No killer, I don't want any trouble." Bryce spoke nervously, his laugh trailing off.

Luckily, my brother was right. He had actually gone on to tell me not to stop hitting Jon until someone had to drag me off of him. That might have been the best strategy, but I hate violence. After that one incident, "the wrecking crew" were nothing more than ghosts to me. I honestly hadn't seen either of them since that very day. What happened to Eric does make me sick, and I would like to help, but I've already fought my own battle with

Jon. Eric is bigger than me, taller, and more muscular anyway, so I'm sure he can fend for himself.

Did Kenneth say that was the tardy bell? Crap I'm going to be so late!!! I walked as fast as possible without being in an actual run. When I got to the stairs, I leaped over the first section, and tried to land as quietly as possible, then leaped from the top of the last section.

"Hey you need to slow down this instant!!" -Ms. April demanded.

"Sorry, just trying to get to class." I blurted nervously.

"Try managing your time more wisely. It will help." Ms. April said condescendingly.

"I will. Thanks Ms. April." I smirked, still moving as fast as possible, without pushing the limited grey area between too fast and acceptable.

Ms. April was every boys' favorite teacher at my school, and the teacher most disliked by every girl student. She had the true Barbie doll look going on. Perhaps a model would have been a more appropriate career path for her judging by appearance alone. I thought as I rushed to class.

Upon entering the gym, I could not believe who was already there. I had hurried there as fast as I could, without severely breaking the rules, and while Mike was still at his locker. Yet, there he was.

"How did you beat me here?" I inquired.

"I walked." -Mike replied laughing.

"Walked? Who are you, some serial killer from a horror movie? Everyone runs from you, and you only walk, yet stay right behind them!" I blurted.

"No. I don't know. I just walked here down the blue hall." Mike marveled.

"I went the same way, but down the other stairs. Just doesn't make any sense though." I stammered.

"I may have taken a little short cut, but I'll never admit to it." Mike said with a sly grin. His secret? Our school is shaped like the top portion of a wing, with the main lobby and offices sitting in the middle like the head of a bird and connecting both sides. Mike had gone down the stairs, then out the emergency exit. Leaving him with only a short distance to walk in a straight line, right into the exit door from the gym.

P.E. is excruciating for the first half hour. One would think our P.E. teacher, Mr. Thomason, was a retired drill Sargent or something. He acted like he was trying to whip us into shape, then sending us off to fight a war in a faraway land. He was short, had a buzz cut, and looked like a body builder. Even his muscles had muscles. Our routine? Sit-ups, push-ups, running laps, jumping jacks, toe touches, wretched shuttle runs, then repeat it all. After that came the fun stuff, dodge ball, basketball, walk, or what me and my friends liked the most, just hanging out and talking while appearing to play, or do whatever everyone else was doing.

"Ok, we need to get together sometime this summer and go exploring in the woods." I suggested.

"Where at?" Mike asked.

"I figured we could just spend the night at Joe's. There are plenty of woods around his house. I might take you all where me and him went during fall break." I beamed excitedly.

"Yeah man, your brother is cool. It was fun getting to drive his truck last summer. How many adults would actually trust us behind the wheel? I mean, we were in a field where little could go wrong, but still." Brady, my cousin, added. Brady was one of a kind…somehow. He was into video games and comic books to a point bordering on addiction. He was really smart, or at least he appeared that way to most of our classmates, including myself. He was like an underrated cool kid or something. For instance, random classmates liked asking his opinion on things, or they would prod him for information about things no other kid our age would know anything about.

"Yes, I do remember Mike got his truck to bunny hopping, just before killing the engine." I chuckled.

"Hey, I did alright after that. I just wasn't used to the clutch in a truck. If it had been a car, I would have been ok!" Mike exclaimed.

"My brother and my dad both have said if you can drive one you can drive the other." I stated, receiving a 'whatever' look from Mike.

"I wanna see that bluff you were talking about. Sounds like a lot of work for one person to do all of that." Brady exclaimed.

"The one with the ladder? Deer stand thing or the other one?" I asked.

"The other one you were talking about, with the fire place." Brady informed.

I had almost forgotten about that one. Joe and I were walking along the top of a hill, and off to one side we noticed a bluff. It was a large thin rock protruding out of the hill, with a path worn out leading under the edge of it. Joe suspected coyote's, or maybe even bob cats, were living under it. Animals entering and exiting would had theoretically caused the path. Going in for a closer look though, we were amazed at the work someone had put into it. Level ground formed underneath. The rock itself was high enough to allow a person of average height to walk upright in the area.

Creek rocks had been carried up a massively steep hill, placed in an inverted funnel shape forming a stove, complete with chimney. Creek rocks bound together by dried mud, presumably from the creek as well, were built all the way up to the topside of the rock bluff. A long bench sat near the back where the bluff began its embedment in the earth, along with a large cooler, cooking utensils for the rock stove, and a hammock hanging down from the rock ceiling. It was a place most anyone would find camping comfortable, aside from using a camper trailer that is.

"Yes, that is a must see!!" I stated.

"When would you all want to do this? This hiking trip?" Mike inquired.

"It isn't exactly hiking. I mean, what comes to my mind when I hear hiking is just walking on a beaten trail. What I'm suggesting is exploration at its finest! Boldly going where potentially no one has gone before, or maybe just not for a long time." I encouraged.

"Here we go again. Look, taking a stroll, walking, hiking, and wandering aimlessly through the woods where there are mosquitos and snakes and all other sorts of things that want to eat us…. Let's face it it's really all the same." Brady debated.

"I agree, but you left out the best part. There could be girls!" Mike spoke with enthusiasm.

"What? Like Sirens?" I asked.

"No. Like out of towners boating on the lake for the fourth of July! If we are going to admire some scenery, I hope there is some scenery to admire!" Mike replied laughing.

"Who says we will be near the lake? Just because we are in the woods doesn't necessarily mean we will be near a lake." Brady pointed out.

"You have a point, but around here, not many areas with woods are far from a lake." Mike responded.

Brady and I were at the age where girls were just confusing to us. Earlier they were just like anyone else, just one of the guys, but lately everything seemed to be…. changing. They seemed to be more difficult to talk to. Not just for the reason of hearing the annoying K-I-S-S-I-N-G song or a random "you got cooties" line. Mike however, seemed to be changing with the times.

"I will check with Joe. As soon as he gets a weekend off of work, I will give you guys a call and we will do it!" I informed them excitedly.

"Sounds good." Brady agreed.

"Yup." Mike stammered, turning his attention to the cheerleaders practicing.

I honestly dreaded this being the last day of school. I'm usually lonely at my house. My parents are old and don't really do much anymore. I'm just there having to entertain myself for the most part. My uncle and Brady visit every now and then, maybe once or twice a month. Sometimes my Uncle takes us to get comic books, or on a rare occasion, to the movies. I like reading comics from time to time, but I'm really fonder of the artwork that goes into creating them, than some of the story lines. Those are always fun times I look forward to, but nothing compares to the sights and findings one encounters whilst in the woods. Now, those are the times I live for.

Last period everyone is gathered in the hallways signing each other's year books. I wasn't able to get one this year, or last year, or the year before that. My parents always say they cost too much money, and they needed their money for more important things. Sometimes it sounded more like one of the excuses I've been accused of using.

My dad? He farms. We have some cows, horses, and he grows crops. One year it will be corn, the next soy beans, always switching it up from year to year. My mom works in a local shirt factory full time, and helps dad with the farm the rest of the time.

Usually the first days of school are a little sad. Most of the kids in my grade have exciting stories to tell of vacations they went on, to fascinating and/or exotic places over the summer. Me? Mine are usually the same.

"Well, I didn't go anywhere or do anything out of the ordinary."

To which the teachers always reply:

"Oh, so you just had a good break from school then. That's what I did. It's nice to get a break even if you don't really go anywhere."

I suppose they are right, but for once I'd love to have a fantastic story ready to go when asked about my summer on the first day of the school year. Things looked promising for this summer. It might not be a world class vacation to faraway lands, but I'm sure the adventure I'm planning for me and my friends will provide one good story worth telling!!

"Shawn, will you sign my year book?" Cary, a smart nerdy girl in my class, asked me.

"Sure. I guess. No one else has asked me to sign theirs. Do you really want me to?" I asked doubtfully.

"Well, yes I am sure I want you to. I'm not everyone else either, so I would be honored if you signed." Cary assured.

"Have a great, and safe summer!! See you next year! Shawn" I wrote in her year book.

"Shawn!! Sign mine as well. I'm trying to get everyone in our class to sign mine! So far you are the only one left, a couple are out today, and three guys refused do it." Amber, a popular and somewhat snobby girl in my class begged.

"Sure." I mumbled, unenthused about the idea. So, I simply signed my name in hers. It made me feel pretty special her wanting me to sign just so she can have everyone's signature- not. Amber, a girl who has never spoken to me until this very moment. I guess my cousin and Mike are the only two friends/associates I really needed anyway.

Before I knew it, school was over. I got on the bus and took my seat in the back, trying to act cool, even though I wasn't. Middle schoolers. We were the next to last to get on the bus. The noise was already a low steady murmur. By the time we reached the high school, the noise level had increased noticeably. I just looked out of my window, watching everyone walking this way and that. The high schoolers looked so important, like they each and every one had some place important to be.

'That will be me next year. First day of school I will have a story, maybe even stories, to tell that will send everyone into a state of awe. They will talk about it with their friends, and several of them will come to me to hear it firsthand. I will be important for a change, slightly more popular than I am now.' I thought.

In the blink of an eye, my long transit was over. The noise had increased drastically when the high schoolers boarded the bus. Seeing my small white home was a pleasant sight amid all of the noisy conversations occurring around me.

"Hurry in and pack." Mom demanded, as soon as I opened the front door.

"Pack? Are we going on vacation!!??" I asked excitedly.

"Oh, of course not. You know we can't afford that. We are moving, silly." Mom chuckled.

"Moving? I don't want to move!! You all can move, and I'll just keep living here on my own!! I don't want to move and have to start a new school! I only have two friends here, and one of them is my cousin Brady." I grunted angrily

"You won't have to change schools. You will keep going to the one here." Mom responded bluntly.

"Then why does everyone else that moves have to change schools? Why do we get new students at random because they moved here? Why wouldn't everyone just keep going to the same school after they had to move somewhere new?" I argued.

"Do you just want to be in trouble? Get your butt to your room right now, and start packing. We are trying to get moved in over the weekend." Mom demanded again.

I stomped into my room, and plopped down on the edge of my bed. I squeezed my mattress in my fists while staring at the floor. Just like that, in the blink of an eye, my grand plan for an awesome adventure this summer was potentially thwarted. What if Uncle George and Brady, maybe even Mike, couldn't find our new house? What then? Mike's parents seemed ok, pretty smart and resourceful. Uncle George though, at times, seemed a little off his rocker. If our new house was going to be difficult to find, my faith in him doing so, was slim.

I hated this news with a passion. It felt like my whole world had been yanked out from underneath my feet in one swift motion. Why couldn't they have at least asked me what I thought about moving to a new house? Does my opinion have no merit at all?

"Shawn!!!" Mom yelled loudly. "You better be packing!!"

2

I turned quickly, looking through my bedroom door, just in time to see several large boxes flying into my room.

"Get started boxing your things! Put your clothes in one or two, and whatever else you have in the others. Your dad will be back any minute to load up the truck again. We will try to get your dresser and wardrobe loaded up and taken over there tonight. I'm hoping tonight will be our first night in our new house." Mom yelled with fury in her voice.

"Will the phone work there?" I asked sadly. If our phone wouldn't work, how would I be able to tell Mike and Brady about moving? If only my parents would change with the times and upgrade to a smart phone, this wouldn't be an issue. Instead, we are stuck with a landline like a bunch of cave people.

"No. The phone people are going to be there around the middle of next week to hook it up." Mom replied, her frustration building.

That's just wonderful news piled on top of everything else. May isn't even over yet, and July is over a month away, but still I need to let my people know what's going on. What if they need to talk to me, and we have no phone? Ok, so that is probably just some wishful thinking, anything is possible though. One unbearable week of isolation, cut off entirely from the outside world. How depressing.

With a sigh, and still pretty upset, I kicked one box over to the dresser. Totally bummed out about my plans quickly fading into the distance with this absurd spur of the moment life changing situation, I begin dumping my clothes into the big box. First my sock drawer, then my undershirts, and tighty whiteys. I wasn't even paying attention to how much was actually going into the box, until mom yelled at me again.

"Son, what in the world are you doing?" She barked, patience wearing thin. I turned my attention to the pile beside me, half in the box, and half on the floor.

"Sorry, mom. I really don't want us to move. How about you and dad move, and I will just stay here?" I begged.

"Absolutely not. Besides you haven't even seen our new house yet. I'm sure you will love it. There is lots of room there. Inside as well as outside. It has a pretty big yard, and a field in the back so you have plenty of room to ride your four-wheeler. I'm sure you will forget all about this place as soon as you see our new one. So, snap out of it and get to packing. Your dad is going to be back any minute." She cheered.

I gathered the disastrous pile in my arms, and dropped it into the box. Soon the task at hand was complete, just in time for my dad to step inside barking orders to get everything loaded. I honestly couldn't figure out what the rush was. They were acting like our lives depended on moving this very night. Wow, they bought a new house, so what? I've got all summer to move after all…. if they would let me take my time anyway.

"Hi dad." I mumbled, carrying an arm load of boxes past him.

"Hi son. Put those in the trunk of your mother's car. We will load the beds up in the back of my truck as soon as I get them taken apart. Hurry, because we are burning daylight." Dad spoke, sternly.

Stepping outside, the sunset caught my eye. A wide-open field lay across the road from the front of our house, with a slight incline of earth at the back side of it. The very tip top of the sun blazed just above the hill. Its rays grasped the freshly bush hogged grass in the field, fighting against its descent, not ready to set just yet. Pinks, purples, yellows, and blues filled the sky, making it appear like a delicate marble. I paused, maybe for too long, just to soak up the sunset. It wouldn't be the last time I saw one, but possibly the last time seeing one this magnificent.

"Son, what part of hurry do you not understand? We are losing day light!" Dad urged, sounding irritated.

"Ok." I mumbled. I had a ton of great memories of this place, and a ton more that I will never get to make. This place is and will always be home, no matter how far away we move.

Only a few weekends ago, Mike rode his horse to my house. On most roads, it would have been a little dangerous, but we live on a one lane road in the middle of nowhere with very, very little traffic. It took us about half the day to just catch my horse. When we finally caught it, and piled the rigging on, we rode in our field. Later, we rode all the way to his house. Horses aren't really my thing; they are simply way too unpredictable. The worst near death experience of my life, to date, was on a horse.

One beautiful, sunny, Saturday morning, I was overwhelmed by the urge to go for a ride. A day with perfect weather, and clear skies as far as the eye could see. The very kind of day that just taunts and beckons one to venture out doors, and dive into some sort of adventure.

At the time, I had a little black pony with a white blazed face, named Bandit. I threw the saddle and all the rigging on him, and hopped on for a mysterious journey. I was riding down to the end of our road, and planned on hitting an old dirt road to the lake. When we were within sight of the dirt road, a group of dogs had managed to creep up behind us from out of the woods. As they closed in, ferocious barking quickly ensued. The sudden outburst of growls, glaring eyes, and sharp teeth startled Bandit.

Next thing I knew, the saddle had slid around, underneath the horse's belly, when he did a half rear up half turn. Somehow, I was dangling upside-down, with my head almost hitting the ground with each step Bandit took. I remained seated firmly on the saddle, somehow defying the laws of gravity, with my feet still in the stirrups squeezing Bandits belly. I held on for dear life as he ran from the dogs. Zigging and Zagging my head, to keep from getting whacked in the face by the horses' massive hooves.

Looking back on it now, it would make for one hilarious cartoon. Of course, it would need to be spruced up with wolves or bears chasing a cowboy. No doubt about it, I do prefer something with a minimum of two wheels, as opposed to a form of transportation barring a mind of its own.

"Hey Shawn, stop whatever you are doing and help me load the mattress and boxed springs." Dad called from the bedroom.

"Sure thing. I'll be right there." I replied from the kitchen. What can I say? I needed a break and had to get a glass of water. Packing, and reminiscing at the same time, is hard work with a one-track mind.

Loading up the head boards, foot boards, and all other bed components, was fun. It seemed like only a matter of seconds had passed when we finally had it all crammed into the bed of my dad's old white truck.

"Honey, you and Shawn follow me in case something falls out. If anything were to fall out, honk the horn, flash your lights, or something." Dad instructed.

"Sure. Help me get the rest of these boxes in my car, and we will call it a night. We can get the beds setup and unpack just what we will need for tonight." She replied, sounding dead tired, wiping sweat from her brow.

Chucking the last of my boxes into the back seat of mom's old car, I slammed the door. I couldn't believe the sun had already gone down. A full moon shined exceptionally bright in the night sky, nearly bright enough to make it appear as day. My parents were still acting very peculiar, rushing nonstop getting everything they thought we would need for our first night. If they had tried to take the kitchen sink, I would not have been the least bit surprised.

"Oh no!! Dan, I have locked my keys in the house! Open the door for me, and then we will be all set." Mom panicked.

"I wish I could. I must have laid my keys down on the table when I got back." Dad replied, after digging in his pockets for a couple of minutes. "I think I might be able to open our bedroom window and get in that way."

"STOPPP!!!! WHY DO WE HAVE TO MOVE??? WHY ARE YOU TWO ACTING SO CRAZY?? WHAT IS GOING ON???!!!!" I yelled at the top of my lungs.

"Stop that yelling, right this instant mister!! Just be quiet and do what we tell you!!" Mom bellowed.

"Shawn, you can ride with me. Just calm down, and let me get our keys, ok?" Dad replied quickly.

"FINE!" I grunted angrily.

Dad slid the window open, eventually, after a good long struggle with the swelled wood framing. Getting it closed again was a task of equal challenge. Moments later, dad popped out the front door and tossed mom her keys.

"Come on kiddo, hop in the truck. We need to be on the road." Dad beckoned.

"So why the hurry?" I asked curiously.

"Well son, for one, our house is small. We don't have a lot of room here. Sure, it's a three bedroom, but they are three tiny bedrooms. Your stuff alone takes up not only your room, but half of your brother's old room as well. Your mom and I have been looking for a bigger house for a long time now. We finally found one that we both agree on. It's not perfect. The land that goes with it isn't exactly ideal, but we did get a really good deal on it. One that we could not pass up. So yes, we are really excited about it. Sure, we could wait about moving in, not be in such a hurry. However, we did have to get a decent sized mortgage, and I just do not want to go one single night without staying there. After all, we are going to have to make payments on it. I just see no reason to pay for something that we are not going to use." Dad spoke cheerfully.

"Waiting about moving in doesn't have anything to do with that. It will be used in time, just not as fast as you all want. Why can't we wait until the phone and everything is working?" I argued.

"Look, our first payment is due in one month. Your mother and I want to get moved in, and then start some work that needs to be done on it. Some of the rooms need to be painted, there is a barn that needs to be cleaned out, storage building that needs cleaned out, and just a lot to do really. Not to mention getting all of our big stuff moved there. Cows, horses, the tractor, other farm equipment, and last but not least, would be your four-wheeler." Dad replied, seeking an end to the conversation.

"Fine, but I still don't like it. You better not sell our house or anything, because when I'm older, I will move right back there." I demanded. Dad patted my shoulder and our conversation ended there. I turned my focus to the fence posts swishing by outside my window. I felt helpless. That's probably an understatement. My current mood was one of far greater helplessness than I had experienced my fourth-grade year at the hands of Jon. My entire world was crushed. Our house was small, ok I give them that, but it was home all the same. I didn't understand it, but it looked like I was just going to have to make the best of it.

The swishing of the fence posts was a gentle lullaby playing in my ear, tugging at my eyelids. Fields containing cows and other variations of livestock, or crops, were scattered along the road like a heavy snow. The sections of fence were separated by homes, or other roads causing a barely noticeable cease in swishes. My head gracefully descended onto my door, atop a lowered window. Cold night air whipped into the cab, and raced through my thick hair, sending cold chills over me. Relaxing, soothing, relentless, drowsiness overcame me.

3

A violent shaking of my bed snapped me from a deep sleep. My eyes remained closed as thoughts of an unsettling dream raced into my conscious mind. 'Moving? No way, it was only a dream.' I thought to myself, pulling the covers tightly around me. My bed began shaking again, more violently than what had awoken me at first. I was terrified. It felt like my bed was falling, picking up massive amounts of speed, then bumping into random objects on the way down a bottomless pit. This caused the springs to bounce frantically.

I pictured in my mind, a strange man at the foot of my bed shaking it. It was as if he were waiting for my eyes to open, and fall on him just before he sliced me up. Then it stopped shaking. Was it a trap? My ears perked up, listening carefully, to catch even the slightest sound… Nothing.

Panic had questions blowing through my mind like a tornado. Should I scream for help? No. Why? The homicidal maniac in my room would probably shove a pillow down on my face, and start stabbing away. Should I try to make a run for it? No, my room is too small and he could easily grab me. What can I do to avoid certain death? I've got it, play dead. If he thinks I'm already dead maybe he will leave, not wanting to waste his time. Oh no!! My parents!! What about them? My dad is tough, strong, and really intimidating. He could handle the bad guy!! Unless, he has already been to their room! Crap!! My heart raced; my playing dead theory has now been compromised. My breathing was no longer controllable…. the moment of truth…I opened my eyes-

"DAAAADDDDDDDDDD!!!!!!!!" I screamed as loud as I possibly can. "DAAADDDD!!!!!!! MOOOOMMM!!!!!"

"Honey what is it?" Mom answered, running into the room.

"Where am I? What's going on? Is that blood on the door??? Where are we???? Where is dad???" I cried.

"This is our new house sweetie. Calm down. You fell asleep on the way here last night, and we didn't want to wake you." She said in her gentle, motherly voice, and held me in her arms.

"My bed!!! My bed was shaking like crazy!!! When I woke up, when I opened my eyes, … I saw the blood on the door!! Did someone die in this house?? In this room??? Why is there blood on the door??!!!" I shrieked.

"Calm down. Your dad and I felt it too. The whole house was shaking. We think it could have been an earthquake. There is no blood on the door either. As far as someone dying in this house? I don't know for sure. There was an elderly couple that lived here before we bought the place. They were taking care of one of their parents and their parent, mother I believe it was, passed away recently. She could've passed here, or in the hospital. I really do not know." She replied in a soothing voice.

"Earthquake?? We've never had an earthquake before. I knew we should never have moved. The door, don't you see the blood on the door?? It's right there!!!" I said frantically, pointing at the dried blood stains.

"Listen sweetie, we are only a few miles away from our old house. Even if we had been there, we still would have felt it. There is a fault line on the western side of our state. The door just has water damage, that is it. We have a leaky roof. There is an upstairs, but the leaky roof has caused some water damage in places. That is one of the things we need to fix soon." She said in her softest voice.

"Water spots?" I asked trying to regain control of myself.

"Yes, that is exactly right. You see how it starts at the top of the door and appears to trickle down? Just like if someone had poured water on the top edge of the door, making it flow down like a waterfall?" Mom asked.

"I guess so. Still looks like blood to me though. I hate this room and never want to be in it ever again!" I stated.

"Very well, there just so happens to be three other bedrooms for you to choose from. Me and your dad like this one, and thought about it being ours anyway. Come on. Let's go eat breakfast. It's almost done, and I need to check on it." She insisted.

"Ok." I answered.

I approached the bedroom door like it was alive, ready to turn into a mouth and swallow me whole. Cautiously, I took the tips of my fingers and flung the door open, back against the inner bedroom wall. To my surprise, and further igniting my initial thought of blood stains, the opposite side of the door was flawless. Perfectly smooth, and snow white. A leaky roof she said. Maybe. But wouldn't' both sides of the door be water damaged? I mean, let's face it, a bedroom door is not going to remain in the same position every minute of every day. Or every single day for that matter. Rain snow or sunshine, it won't be in the exact same position. My opinion remained, it was blood.

I stepped out of the bedroom and found myself in a hallway. A long, dark, narrow stretch of ugly lime green linoleum floor. It was bordered with the same color wall paper. My mom had disappeared so quickly I didn't see which way she had gone upon exiting the bedroom. To my left, I could see a room with a red carpet. After my experience waking up and seeing the door, I just wasn't up for exploring any room with red in it. To my right, I noticed two doors staggered along the hall on opposite sides, with what appeared to be a larger opening at the very end of the hall. Hmmm, Should I investigate door number one? Door number two? I didn't think so, not this instant anyway. Closed doors can simply stay closed, as far as I'm concerned. Walking carefully toward the opening, I heard the faintest of foot steps behind me. I paused, glancing over my shoulder I found an empty dim hall. Terrified of what could be in front of me now, I slowly turned my head back to face forward praying nothing was there. A sigh of relief fell from my lips as I only stared into the same empty hall. I began walking once again. Cold chills swarmed my body as the faint footsteps, paced down the hall, barely out of sync with my own. Could it be my steps echoing along the hall giving the illusion of another person? Perhaps. I stopped just past the door to my left, and not yet in front of the door to my right. My ears listened for the footsteps sounding behind me. I was frozen stiff, heart beating so hard I felt it hammering in my chest.

I heard one step, just inches behind me, I ran as if my life depended on it toward the opening. Stepping into the opening, I glimpsed my mom at a kitchen sink to the left. Stepping again, I spun in the air, and landed with my back against the wall. Peering back down the dark hallway I see…. nothing at all.

"Honey, seriously, it is only water damage on the door. Relax a little. If you want, I will have your dad bring your four-wheeler over soon so you can ride around outside. Will that get your mind off of the ugly door?" Mom grunted.

"I don't know. Something isn't right with this house. I just know it." I pleaded.

"Believe me, I know it. I was looking upstairs earlier and they have left a huge mess up there that we need to clean up. I've found a lot here that needs fixed or cleaned, so that is all we are doing for the next week or two." Mom replied sarcastically.

"Next week or two?? I have things I wanna do sometime this summer. I do not want to spend it all cleaning a creepy old house that I didn't want to move into in the first place." I begged.

"I don't know what your problem is, but you really need to get in a better mood. You need to just accept the fact that we have a new house…new to us anyway." Mom replied, letting me know it was time to be quiet.

Two weeks trying to clean up the creepy dead house was not how I wanted to begin my summer. I would much rather have my adventure as soon as possible, despite Mike wanting to do it around the fourth of July. I was ready to perfect my incredible summer story.

Adding to my melancholy, after breakfast we got to work, which might actually work out for the best. If we hurried and got everything done, hopefully it would only take a week, or less, preferably. We unpacked merely the essentials. Mom and I took on the smaller tasks, while dad tackled the larger ones. At the end of the first day, all of the hideous wall paper had been stripped from the walls, with exception of the hallway. It, for some reason, was untouched and not on any to-do list of theirs.

Day two was more strenuous by far, and set the pace for the days to come. All random items that had been left behind, were bagged up, and I was nominated to be the work horse lugging them out into the back yard, to be burned later. Four huge trash bags were quickly filled with items from upstairs, and tossed down for me to carry out.

'Surely it's time for lunch by now.' I thought on my way back inside. I was under the impression that was the last of what was upstairs. I was hopeful for a sandwich, or better yet, a nice big cheese burger would really hit the spot.

"Shawn, I'm going to fix some lunch. I left three more bags of trash upstairs you need take out before you eat." Mom ordered.

"Sure thing." I replied dreadfully.

"Oh, and be careful on those steps!! They are tricky. Way too tall, and small." She yelled as I passed by her.

Standing at the bottom of the steps I realized what she meant. They were an awful design, and structure. Whoever built them must have been a giant, with the feet of an infant. I held on to the railing tightly as I climbed to the top. Half way up, I decided against carrying the trash bags down. That would be almost certain death, a few broken bones, or just a bloody mess.

At the top of the steps I found the trash bags sitting to the right. I turned and tossed them down, then looked around the room. This was first time I had been up here, and was not impressed at all. It was nowhere near finished. Only one small light was positioned above the stairs. The interior was comprised of rough walls, without paneling or sheetrock, no insulation, and rough splintery boards for the floors and ceiling. I had seen barn lofts that were in better shape than this, believe it or not. I know that sounds contradictory since I'm afraid of heights. I imagine whoever built the barn at our old house had the same fear, because they had made stair steps to get up to the loft.

Turning to look at the other side, I saw a doorway. Beyond that, there was another room of equal size, another doorway with a large window posing as a door for a third room of equal size. The room in which I stood, and the next room, still had lots of clutter. But there was something in the last room. Something beyond the window that held my attention. My eyes strained, trying to focus amid the darkness, and figure out what it was that I was seeing, what it was… that was …moving back there.

"Shawn, hurry up please. Lunch is almost done!!" Mom called from the kitchen.

"I'll be down in a second!" I yelled back. At the sound of her voice I turned to look down the stairs. After my response, I turned my attention back to the window door. Something was in motion, ever so slightly back there. What was it? It almost looked like something… hanging, swaying slightly from side to side. I stepped closer. I couldn't make it out. Poor lighting made visibility almost impossible all the way back there. I stepped closer, and a little closer. Now almost in the doorway. Then I heard it. The horrid twisting sound of an old rope holding something heavy. I take another step, stopping just inside the doorway. The sound of the rope twisting continued. I noticed something in the darkness out the corner of my right eye. I turned my head for a better visualization.

'…A trash bag??? Who would hang up a trash bag?' I thought. The gently swinging object made its way over into the light, and stopped way off center.

'Long, thin, stringy, oily… hair, appeared resembling that of a coconut, and floated peacefully out into the air. A mannequin maybe? Were the last residents fashion designers?' I thought to myself. The thought brought a smile to my face, until I heard a foot firmly plant itself on the floor amidst the darkness. I noticed the bag turning slowly, leaning more outward into the light. A grotesque woman, wearing an ankle length midnight blue dress with tiny white polka dots, hung from a traditional thirteen coil hangman's noose. Her head slowly raised up, and twisted around on a crackling neck to face me. Deep wrinkles formed below her lips, and the remaining flesh on her badly rotting face. Dark hollow sockets, lacking eyeballs, now peered into the depths of my soul, somehow holding me inert for the longest moment.

I jumped back, unable to look away as a fleshless right hand flew up, grabbing for me. Her mouth dropped open. Slimy maggots poured from her coarsely, wrinkled, decaying mouth, and slithered on the splintery floor boards. A foul smell filled the air. Vomit flooded my mouth with the first whiff of rotting flesh in the humid loft, penetrating my nostrils. Before she could speak, I ran back to the stairs and began a careless descent, almost falling. As I regained my balance halfway down, I looked behind me- Nothing. I peeked above the loft floor toward the doorway, nothing. All I saw was a white bag of concrete mix hanging in the darkness. '

"That can't be right." I mumbled, and returned to the doorway, only to find just that. A white bag of mix, half empty and swaying back and forth in the darkness. Bound only by a thin silver wire. "Am I losing my marbles or something? She was right here!!" Looking down at the floor, one tiny maggot was crawling around, and slipped between two floor boards.

"Mom, have you noticed anything weird here? Footsteps? Dead women hanging from a noose? Anything that just doesn't make any sense?" I asked before taking a bite of pizza.

"No, I have not. But as busy as we have been, I haven't had time to notice much of anything other than more things that need work." Mom replied, using her matter-of-fact tone.

"What about dad? Has he noticed anything out of the ordinary?" I asked curiously.

"I think he said you and him are going to have to repair the fence on the back side of the pasture before he can move the livestock." Mom stated.

"That's not what I meant." I said depressingly. Why can't they take me seriously for once? I know I'm not the only one this is happening to, am I?

Late in the evening, we finally had all of the trash, or items being trashed, removed from the upstairs. The main floor was also cleared of miscellaneous items left behind by the previous owners. All of the wreckage from mom and dad's interior design plans, had been taken out as well. I guess it made sense to them, but totally went against their "Leave well enough alone." motto. After dinner, I went out on the deck to relax on the porch swing and read a book.

Sunset. Not much of a view of a sunset here. At this house, the sun sets on down the road, far enough away that we only got to see short streaks of the glorious colors over the tree tops. A view only good for arousing one's suspicions to see more, to see what lay just beyond the tree tops and massive hill that hid a most pleasing splendor.

4

Slipping from this reality, and into another. Journeying with a boy and his dogs, right into a brutal fight with a mountain lion. As the tension rises, I read even faster to see what would happen to him and his hounds. Just then, a loud old car with squeaking brakes, pulled into the driveway costing me my temporary escape from the dead house.

"Hey sonny! Yer folks home?" An old bald-headed man asked from his old sedan, in a high-pitched voice.

"They are inside, I'll go and get them." I answered.

I closed my book and went inside. Mom and dad were in the kitchen drinking coffee, and talking about further plans for the house.

"Hey some old guy is outside asking for you two." I informed.

"Who is it?" Dad asked from his chair at the kitchen table.

"Never saw him before. Some old bald guy in a long red car. Kind of looks like a land yacht." I replied shrugging my shoulders. Dad got up and went outside. I took a seat in the living room and flipped on the TV. 'Great. The cable guys are probably running behind, along with the phone guys.' I thought to myself.

"Oh hey, come on in and grab a seat. Do you all want some coffee or anything?" Dad bellowed excitedly, standing in the doorway. "Hey Cheryl, you remember Lloyd and Marge, don't you?"

"How could I forget? They gave us such a good deal on this house." Mom replied, getting two more coffee mugs out of the cabinet. "How do you all like your coffee? Or would you like something else to drink?"

"Oh, coffee is fine dear. Lloyd likes his with cream and sugar, straight black for me please." Marge said as the couple entered the living room. Her and Lloyd had obviously doused themselves in putrid fragrances before they arrived here. Their stench sent my sense of smell into overload. Every last drop of saliva in my mouth vanished the instant the aroma hit me like a bag of bricks. With my mouth as dry as sandpaper, I ran to the kitchen for water.

Lloyd made me a little paranoid with his attire. Brown trousers, highly polished milk chocolate loafers, white button-up shirt, and a dress coat made from the same fabric as our twenty-year-old sofa. All of it combined gave him the look of a sleazy used car salesman. The type of car salesman that would knowingly sell someone a pile of junk, blaring snow white teeth behind a sly grin during the process. Then stand in front of the car lot, waving, smiling the same sly grin, as it breaks down the moment you get on the highway. As your anger flares, realizing you purchased a lemon, the salesman has vanished without a trace the instant you look back.

Large bifocals rested on top of his short pudgy nose. He had a pot belly, big giant elephant ears, and was bald except for a small portion of grey hair barely stretching around the lower back of his head.

Marge was equally weird in appearance. Her facial expressions screamed "I stuck my finger in a light socket right before we drove here, with my head hanging out of the window, while Lloyd accelerated to Mach three." She had exceptionally large eyes, and a smile that ran from ear to ear. Her hair was silver and curly, really curly. It was as if a big silvery snow ball was encapsulating her head. She was clothed in a low-cut black dress, with clashing colorful flowers, and white high heels. Heels that I only imagine to be a safety hazard for a woman of her age. She wore big ugly rings on every finger. Cheap ones from the looks of it, as they had turned her fingers as green as the rings were themselves.

'Where in the world are these people from?' I thought to myself. They spoke using bizarre accents that I had not heard before. A tone so…. odd, they could easily pass for aliens off of a Sci-Fi flick.

"So, what brings you all back to this part of the woods?" Dad asked casually, as the strange couple joined them at the kitchen table.

"No reason really. Marge just wanted to visit here one last time. Say our goodbyes to this ole place basically. It's funny how people grow so attached to things over time. Selling a house is almost like cutting off an arm or leg…almost like losing her head in matter of speaking." Lloyd joked.

"Yeah, I'm sorry for the intrusion. I hope we aren't interrupting anything." Marge apologized.

"Of course not. You all are more than welcome here any time. I know how it is, so visit as much as you like. We still haven't met any of the neighbors. I think we know most of them already, but there are some we don't know." Mom replied in an understanding voice.

"Actually, I was thinking today that I would like to talk to you all again. Just to get a better understanding of the property line, and I have a few questions about the wiring for the barn." Dad added.

"It works out good then. I can help ye with all of that. Let's step outside before it gets completely dark and I'll show ye where the line runs, and we can talk about the barn." Lloyd suggested.

Dad and the Lloyd man walked outside. I decided to go sit in the kitchen with mom and the Marge lady. I poured a tall glass of orange juice, and sat down at the table, facing the hallway entrance. As mom and Marge delved into typical small talk and basic chit chat, Marge began acting strange.

At first everything seemed normal. Just your two average adults conversing over some hot steaming coffee. I listened intently, hoping to hear some good intel about this house, but it was not happening. With my attention span burning up with great haste, Marge did something that merited my attention.

Halfway through a sentence about the flower beds, Marge stopped talking, leaving her mouth hanging open. Her face turned snow white. She fidgeted with her mug uncontrollably, and peered down the dark hall with her large eyes.

"Marge?......Hey…. Marge… are you ok?" Mom asked worriedly. I looked down the hall, only finding darkness. It did feel like we were being watched, though nothing could be seen. Mom got up from our table, her eyes locked on Marge, carefully inching toward the frightened lady. Fear was carved into mom's face. Her mouth was hanging open a little, her eyes big, and hands shaking just in front of her like she was feeling her way through a dark room.

"Marge?" She whispered standing beside the woman. Mom gasped as though something cold had touched her back, swiftly brushing her back with her right hand. Her head turned slowly toward the hall. I didn't know what to think. Did they just lose their marbles? Both women were now locked into some kind of trance, or a state of shock, looking at absolutely nothing as far as I could tell.

After several minutes had passed, I was beyond creeped out. Turning the hall light on seemed to be the best solution, though I was having flashbacks of the dead woman upstairs. Getting up from the table, I moved cautiously as my mom had. I kept my eyes glued to the ugly green floor, trying not to see whatever it was that had them so spellbound. Now standing at the edge of the darkness, I lifted my arm, frantically feeling for the light switch. Cold chills trickled down my back, at the sound of a twisting rope breaking the silence. "Found it!!!" I stammered, still looking at the floor with my eyes squinted. Right as I flicked the light on, I felt another hand grab my wrist.

"What are you doing?" Marge asked curiously.

"Oh, ...umm… You were asking for more coffee. I just stepped over here to get your mug." Mom said nervously.

"Oh, right. What were we talking about? Yes!! The flower beds. The flowers I have planted in the back only bloom every other year. So, when they don't bloom this summer, just remember they are flowers. They are delightful. I would just hate you pulling them up thinking they were weeds." Marge informed.

I couldn't believe how flipping the switch had also snapped them out of whatever state they were in, or how whatever had grabbed my wrist was suddenly gone as the dim light came on. How had their conversation simply picked back up from where it left off? I didn't know what they had seen, nor did I want to.

With them back to acting normal, I grabbed my juice and went into the living room. It was dark, illuminated by two small lamps at either end of the room in opposing corners. Sitting in our big fluffy chair with my legs hanging over the arm, I resumed my book. Mom and Marge's voices soon drifted away, far out of my hearing range, as I became immersed in my book hoping to forget about earlier.

As my luck would have it, getting only a few pages farther along, my parents and the elderly couple had gathered into the living room. Loud laughter, cackling, giggling, and other annoying noises erupted every few minutes from Lloyd and Marge. Only brief, peaceful seconds, filled the void in between the insane outbursts. Which, made a steady roar as they talked over each other. Wondering how one could hear what another was saying while also speaking was a world record sized bewilderment.

'I give up.' I thought to myself, closing my book and laying it on the end table beside the little lamp. I curled up on the comfy chair, and closed my eyes. Toning them out completely proved a challenge I could not conquer. Sure, I suppose I could just go get in my mom and dad's bed, which, compared to this environment, might not be a bad idea. The door though, I wasn't ready to see it again. Not just yet anyway. My bed? It's still in pieces, stashed in a couple different rooms at the moment. Between the blood-stained door, creepy hallway, and the room with the red as blood carpet…I'll keep sleeping in the living room, after all, because it is closest to the exit in case, I need to run out screaming 'HELP!! THE GHOSTS ARE COMING!!!'

On and on they went about how times were when they were younger. Followed up by trying to figure out who all they knew, and how those people were related. My parents being noticeably younger, apparently knew and grew up with the sons, daughters, nieces, nephews, and grandchildren of the people the elderly couple had grown up with. I found it all pretty boring. I guess old, or perhaps older, people enjoyed talking a lot about random trivial things.

The conversation progressed increasingly to more pointless subjects. 'God please help me go to sleep.' I begged silently. Loud, obnoxious, sporadic, noisy outbursts continued relentlessly, pounding on my aching head like a sledge hammer. I glanced at our old grandfather clock across the room. 'Great, almost two hours they've been doing this. Don't old people ever get tired of talking?' I thought.

Suddenly, nearing the height of my desperation, their conversation slowed taking a peculiar turn that smacked me into attention.

"Have you all seen Martha yet?" Lloyd asked.

"Oh, no. We have been way too busy with moving. We haven't actually been able to talk to any of the neighbors." Mom answered.

"Where does Martha live? I may have seen her outside when I've been unloading things." Dad asked.

"Lloyd, I know where this is going, and I wish you would just hush about it." Marge blurted hatefully.

"I just thought I would ask. Who knows, maybe you aren't crazy. I still think you are, but all women are a little." Lloyd joked.

"Did I miss something here?? Who is, or where is this Martha??" Mom asked, getting frustrated.

"How old was she dear? Ninety-seven?" Lloyd questioned.

"No, she had her birthday a week before she passed away. She was ninety-eight, dear." Marge informed.

"That is right. It's been so long ago I had forgotten about that. You see, Martha was Marge's mother. Aw, well it is your story Hun, and you do tell it best." Lloyd started.

"Darn tootin' it's my story. I don't think these folks want to hear it, though." Marge grunted.

"I don't follow you all at all. Who is this Martha already???" Dad demanded.

"Well, you see Dan, Martha lived here with us the last few years of her life. One night, Marge… Marge do you wanna take it from here?" Lloyd started again.

"Fine. One night, several months after Mom died, I woke up and had to use the bathroom. I had to go pretty bad, so I wasn't wasting any time getting there. When I stepped into the kitchen, and reached for the bathroom door knob, I saw her by the sink. 'Up for a late-night snack?' I asked her. 'I can't sleep, and thought I'd get a sandwich and lay back down. Would you like one?' she replied. 'Yes, that sounds good mom. After I use the bathroom, I'll fix us some coffee. What kind of sandwiches are you making?' I replied. 'Ham and hot cheese.' She said. 'Fine, fix me one and I'll be right back.' I told her, then hurried into the bathroom. I didn't think much about it until I was washing my hands. It hit me when I turned off the faucet, mom is dead. She can't be in the kitchen!!" Marge said with another annoying cackle.

"How did she die? Did she die upstairs? Hang herself by any chance?" I interrupted.

"Oh, heavens no, she died of old age. She fell terribly ill, and spent just over a week in the hospital. Her heart was too weak and worn out for her to pull through. Doctors said they had done everything they could do, a couple days before she passed. Her last couple of days with us, they kept her medicated so she wasn't in pain, and could leave us peacefully." Marge answered, tears filling her big round eyes. "Anyway, that night, soon as I realized mom was gone… I took a deep breath and opened the bathroom door. There, on the counter at the sink were two plates, and two coffee mugs. The mugs were empty. On one of the plates was a freshly made ham and hot cheese sandwich. The other plate held only bread crumbs, and tiny bits of ham. I don't know how, but she was here that night, in that very kitchen."

"I still say you are crazy as a loon woman!! I think ye made both of those yerself! You probably ate one while half asleep, then used the bathroom and just thought it was her. I never saw her after she died, not once. I'm not nutty like Marge here. Not that I would want to see that old hag anyway." Lloyd blurted, as a strange grouchy expression crept over his face.

"I know what happened!! I know what I saw, and saw what I saw, and it is just like I said it happened!!" Marge yelled at Lloyd, and smacked his leg really hard.

"Crazy woman, plain crazy. How bout you son? You been seein' Martha round here?" Lloyd asked with a hint of anger in his voice.

"I did see a dead woman upstairs. She was in the second room hanging from a noose. She looked awful, and smelled…oh the smell!! (I shivered as nausea started creeping up again) I bet it was her. What about the hallway?? Have you heard the extra footsteps in the hallway???" I spoke eagerly, trying to put this puzzle together.

"Everyone, please calm down. Son, I do not believe in ghosts. I know the move here was sudden, and you are still adjusting to it. Same way Marge went through a major life changing experience. I believe your minds are, or in Marge's case were, playing tricks on you. Furthermore, are you two trying to tell us that you sold us a haunted house? I did not see that, not even in the fine print! Though my disbelief in ghosts is firm, that bit of information might have been nice to have known beforehand." Dad insisted, getting a little upset.

"Believe in ghosts or not Dan, you have one here somewhere. Even if you haven't seen her yet, you will in good time. I saw her, right in there. Maybe that is where you will see her, maybe not. Maybe she was upstairs when sonny boy over there thought he saw her." Marge stated coldly.

"Would you have bought this place knowing this old bat saw a ghost here?" Lloyd asked, flashing the sly grin of a car salesman.

"I think the two of you should leave. We believe in feeding a child's imagination in positive ways, not with this garbage." Mom blurted.

"Ha ha ha!!!! Now we are havin some fun!! I love this! Good times, good times!!!" Lloyd joked.

"You heard the woman, it's time to go. Besides, it is getting late, and we still have a ton of unpacking to do in the morning." Dad ordered.

"Mom, Dad, you have to admit something weird is going on with this house!! I don't think it's that hard to believe!! It all makes sense, sort of. I mean, I did see a woman upstairs, this very morning…she had a noose around her neck, which doesn't support their story of her dying in the hospital. But I know I saw a ghost all the same!" I blurted quickly.

"Son, that is enough. Lloyd, Marge, it has been a pleasure. Now you should leave. Cheryl and I have asked nicely. The next time I have to ask, I will not as polite!" Dad belted.

"You can't be serious. We are just now starting to have fun!!" Marge pleaded, as an evil grin stretched across her wide mouth.

"Yeah, I can't believe we are getting kicked out of our own house!" Lloyd barked, face turning a deep red.

"Get out of MY house! We bought it, and your name is no longer on the deed!! And don't let the door hit you on the way out!!" Mom said angrily.

"Fine, fine. We are going." Lloyd replied just as angrily.

"I've had about enough of you two. Get out already!!" Dad erupted.

I watched as Lloyd and Marge clumsily got to their feet, hobbling out the door on their old legs. Lloyd paused in the doorway, seeking to get in just one last word. Making eye contact with dad, dad shook his head slightly as an indication for Lloyd to think again.

"Too bad they didn't get to hear about Susan. It would be a shame if they went the same way as she did. Maybe they should go exactly like she did, with a little help from us!!" Marge yelled to Lloyd from the driveway.

Lloyd, still locked into a stare down with dad, dropped his head down a little. He lingered, and exhaled a short sigh through his fading grin. Suddenly, the door slammed shut hard enough to make the wall shake, and knocked Lloyd out into the yard on his back. I'm no genius. My guess is the ghost slammed the door, not caring much for Lloyd or Marge. Then again, maybe it was just wanting to help us out rather than having a personal grudge.

Confused about the whole situation, what was going on here? Mom and Marge were stone cold statues only hours earlier, facing the dark hall from the kitchen. How could they not remember anything at all? Dad has been running around aimlessly from one broken item to the next with repairs, upgrades, unpacking, loading, and unloading our stuff. I can see how he could miss some of the things that have occurred, mom on the other hand, doesn't really have that. I mean she kind of does, but she has been inside the entire time. She has to remember what happened in the kitchen earlier doesn't she?? What was Marge yelling at Lloyd before they finally left??? Her voice, though screaming, was not loud enough for me to hear.

"Son, you are not hearing more footsteps in the hall other than your own. The hall is long, so the sound echoes down, getting amplified along the way. What you are hearing is simply that. If the hall is sticky, such as when you mom has finished moping, with bare feet, the sound of skin ripping away from the linoleum is loud. It carries and echoes. That is honestly all it is." Dad stated.

"I hadn't thought of it that way. I guess it makes sense." I replied, putting some thought into his perspective.

"Hey, let's do an experiment. You stand in the kitchen, and I will stand at the other end of the hall. I will speak to you using a normal voice. In that distance, if sounds don't carry like I say it will, then my theory is wrong. But, if it's right, then you cannot believe you heard extra footsteps." Dad insisted.

"Ok, fair enough." I agreed, taking my spot in the kitchen. Dad walked down the hall and stood just inside the room with the red carpet.

"You can hear me loud and clear, can't you?" Dad asked.

"I'm thinking of a number between one and ten, the number 8." I asked in a whisper. "What did I just... "

"Number between one and ten, and it is the number 8 you are thinking of. How's that? Proof enough for you? It did sound like you were standing right beside of me when you spoke." Dad replied quickly.

"I suppose, but I'm still sleeping on the couch tonight." I blurted out, taking a leave to the comfy sofa.

5

"Dan! Are you busy? I need you in the bedroom for a minute." Mom shouted the next morning, waking me from a wonderful sleep.

Not sure where dad was, I figured I would go see what she wanted. Wiping my eyes, I dreaded leaving the living room. It had basically become my safe haven for the past week… well just over a week to be exact, today was Saturday. As my luck would have it, the phone, nor the cable guys had shown up yet, so all of the good Saturday morning cartoons were being watched by everyone but me.

Entering into the creepy hall, I saw dad at the other end. I guess he had been in the basement doing something. Nevertheless, I continued on less terrified knowing he was near.

"What is it Cheryl? I've got my hands full with everything else you have found that needs changed, repaired, or otherwise altered." Dad said, sounding more pitiful than hateful.

"It's this door. I don't know what is going on, if it's the paint, or if I'm painting it wrong. I'm all out of ideas." Mom grunted.

"Is it the color of paint you don't like? You did pick it out." Dad replied, still standing in the hall outside of the bedroom.

"No, the color is fine. It's just not covering these water spots. Seriously, I've put about ten coats of paint on it, and these stupid water spots keep showing through. Not only showing through, it's like I haven't painted over it at all." Mom bellowed.

Dad and I stepped inside, and looked to see what she was talking about. On the inside, a pearl white door that was spotless, shining, twinkling from sunlight pouring in from the window, totally flawless except for the blood stains.

"Maybe it is blood stains?" I suggested. Mom and dad both looked at me with confused facial expressions.

"Blood stains? No son, It's water damage. Maybe we should get some different paint, or maybe we could just find a new door. What do you want me to do Cheryl?" Dad asked.

"I think we should go ahead and do both. New paint, and new door. I hate spending more money on this place, but I really think we should do both." Mom replied sadly.

"Ok. I'm going to finish up a couple things in the basement, then I'll get some measurements, and go try to find a new one. What kind of paint do you want? Same color, different brand?" Dad assured.

"Love you. You are the best babe. Always reading my mind." Mom spoke happily.

"Hey dad, can I go with you? I'd love to get out of here for a while." I begged.

"Yeah, but make sure you are ready to go in about twenty-five minutes. If you aren't, then I'll leave without you." Dad stated.

Walking back to the living room to put my shoes on, I thought about what mom had said. "...about ten coats of paint..." That many should be enough to cover anything. Also, wouldn't water damage be visible on the wall or ceiling above the door? It didn't make any sense to me.

"Ready bub?" Dad asked.

"Yeah, I'm ready to get as far away from here as possible. Even for only a little while." I replied, following him out of the house.

We first stopped by an old antique store that dealt in a wide variety of items. They had basically anything you could dream of, antique wise anyway. We only found five doors there, but none were of the size requirements we needed. The next stop was a larger building supply store. I decided to wait in the truck. It was a nice day with lots of activity outside.

People are strange creatures. Many customers were coming and going. Big families, small families, all behaving as individuals do. Some parents screamed at their young kids to stay close when they were running in the middle of the road. Others, walked together in tight knit groups.

I saw one man who was very suspicious in appearance as well as actions. His green camouflage clothes were tattered and dirty. Maybe he was homeless? His bald head was scarred, and his bony face was fraught with anger. Eyes full of determination, hinting of violence.

Approaching the main entrance, he stopped in front of parking lot traffic. Throwing his hands high in the air, he shook his head aggressively. Suddenly he stopped, lowered his hands, and walked back in the direction he had traveled. Losing sight of this guy, I moved around in the truck, trying to regain some visualization. Several minutes passed. I continued looking every which way, and even through the other car windows parked on either side.

'He's long gone.' I thought to myself. I turned my attention back to the main entrance watching for my dad to come out. After seeing that weird guy I was ready to leave.

"He's back!" I blurted out to myself.

The stranger had made his way back to the main entrance. Head shaking, arms flailing in the air without reason, as he stood in the doorway. Random customers passed by him unscathed, and acting as though nothing of this manner were occurring.

Stopping once more, I expected him to disappear into the parked vehicles as he did moments ago. Instead, he began pacing from the doorway out into the parking lot traffic. He looked angrier than before, stomping the pavement, pacing, and smacking himself in the head for the next quarter hour. One strange performance occurring for all to see, yet going unnoticed by those on foot. However, cars and trucks of all sorts yielded to this mental ward escapee.

Witnessing all of the people walking by him, their total avoidance, complete lack of acknowledgement of this lunatic, soon had me questioning my own psychological state. Could I possibly be, all things considered, seeing another ghost? He was not moving as the woman did upstairs, though his movements were strange nonetheless. Why were random customers passing by him as though they did not have a care in the world?

"Thanks for helping me carry it out, I really appreciate it." Dad said to the store employee. "Ready to head back home son?"

"Yeah, hey, do you see that guy over there?" I asked, hoping desperately for a yes answer.

"I saw him. He must be on drugs. Either that, or something is wrong with him mentally." Dad concluded.

Dad closed his door, and began fishing his truck keys out of his pocket. I looked back one last time at the strange man. He was gone, nowhere in sight. Maybe he finally decided to walk into the store? Hopefully, not acting psychotically like moments ago. If he was, a tornado blowing through the isles would be less devastating than him in his current state.

"So, son, I think it is time for you to pick out a bedroom. I know our couch is broken in, and very comfortable and all, but your bed would be much better for you. In your bed, you would be able to stretch out, have a lot more room, and simply rest better overall. Your mother and I were discussing it last night. We both think you would like the room in the back, the one with the red carpet, the best." Dad demanded, in a suggestive way.

I knew it. I knew this conversation was coming. I didn't know exactly when, but by the way they had been acting, I knew it was inevitable.

"I don't like the carpet in there. It is blood red and creeps me out." I mumbled.

"Ok. So, what about the room with the blue carpet?" Dad asked.

"No, it looks like a dungeon since we tore the white wall paper down. The black walls make it look like.... well, a dungeon. If I have to sleep in there you might as well go ahead and throw some chains and shackles on me." I argued.

"That only leaves one other room, aside from the one you hated because of the water damaged door. Your mom and I took that bedroom." Dad replied.

I had only seen the last room from outside its door. What I had seen inside of it made my stomach gurgle. My face went pale seeing the inner walls stretch, warp, wobble, sway, and bow inward and outward, almost like looking into another dimension through a vaporized portal.

"Let me think about it, and I will figure out which room I want." I said, hoping to get the subject changed to something other than the dead house.

"Great!! Sounds like a plan!! Don't take too long, though. Your mom wants to get your bed setup, and start unpacking your things by this evening. No more sofa for you." Dad beamed, reaching over and giving my ribs a tickle.

Fighting off the laughter was impossible. Reluctant as I was, I caved and laughed until I cried. My laughter died the very second his fingers left my ribs. Having to decide on a room, TODAY, was simply depressing. I reviewed my options. A dungeon. Ok, so it sounds cool, but it was the closest bedroom to the stairs. A ghost, if there really was one up there, could easily slither down the steps, down the hall an extremely short distance, and be right inside. Not something I wanted to risk. Next up, the room with the blood red carpet. It was the largest of the other two, so that was a plus. It was located right beside my parent's room, giving it some bonus points, and taking a couple points away for the same reason. It contained a window with a decent view of the back yard. However, it, along with the last room up for grabs, were sitting right on top of a partial basement. What if the floors were too weak to support my weight? If I fell through, I know I would sustain many broken bones. Deduct twenty points for that reason alone. Lastly, a creepy psychedelic room in another dimension...not a chance.

"So, did you boys have a good trip? Talk about anything interesting?" Mom asked, with excitement in her eyes.

"It was ok mom. There was some weirdo at the hardware store. He acted like he wanted to go in, but couldn't, then started smacking himself in the head like a crazy person." I replied, hoping to avoid the coming conversation.

"Yeah, he must have been fried pretty good to be acting the way he was." Dad stated.

"Goodness, that is just terrible. People need to see stuff like that, see what drugs can do to a person before they start using. Maybe then there wouldn't be so many hooked on them." Mom sympathized.

"It is sad. On to a better subject, we should have a decision later on today. Shouldn't we son?" Dad insisted.

In no way did I understand how that was a better subject. Better for them, I'm sure, but me? Not so much. My life could very well be on the line by choosing poorly in this matter. Possibly the world's scariest game show of pick one of these three doors. Pick the right one and live, pick either of the other two…. you will be doomed!!!! Now a short break from our sponsors….

A simple choice that could result in some dire consequences. I wished it was simple. I've been out of school a whole week now…...and now an idea was forming in my mind.

"Ok, I will have a room picked out by tonight, on one condition." I began.

"Sure buddy. What is it?" Dad questioned.

"If Brady can sleep over tomorrow night. I think it's a fair deal." I reasoned.

"No. We still have a ton of things to do here, and our phone still isn't hooked up. I can't call and see what their plans are for tomorrow night, so that's a no-go Shawn." Mom said pitifully.

"Let's just drive to Uncle George's house tomorrow. We all have been working pretty hard getting moved in here, so we all do deserve a little break. Plus, it will benefit us having Brady here. He can help us out some tomorrow, then me and him can hang out before he goes home." I pleaded.

"He makes a good point dear. An extra person would come in handy. We still haven't mowed the yard, and they could tackle that." Dad added.

"Two against one? Whose side are you on Dan?" Mom replied, faking irritation. "Well, since I seem to be out numbered here...fine. We will drive down there tomorrow, but you have to pick a room tonight, and get your stuff all moved in and unpacked before bedtime!!"

"Yes! I will, no problem there!! Thanks mom!!!" I said with excitement.

Still, my current situation remained the same. I couldn't decide between the dungeon or red-carpet room. A dungeon for a bedroom would be really cool, igniting envy in my friends- what very few I had. ...but I wasn't into the whole emo thing. I guess I could be. I think horror movies and stories are cool. Maybe I could throw up some horror movie posters on the walls… It was as if I could hear the ticking of the clock, pressure building intensely on my decision...I decided to just flip a coin. Heads I take the red room, tails I get the dungeon.

I slipped a quarter from my pocket. I gave it a good flick into the air. The spinning silvery coin climbed higher with each rotation, nearly grazing the freshly painted living room ceiling. Then it quickly fell into my palm. With a twist of my wrist it, splattered onto the back of my left hand. I inhaled deeply, closed my eyes, and lifted my hand off of it. I paused, not wanting to see which room would soon be my demise. I had no preference in this matter, both were equally nauseating. For a few more moments I stood, eyes shut, heart beating in my throat, and the second hand on the clock ticked louder with every passing second.

"If you don't keep your end of the deal, don't expect us to! Time's a wastin." Mom grunted, brushing past on her way to help dad with the new door.

Before I realized it, I had uncontrollably opened my eyes upon forming a response in my mind.

"Guess I'll be sleeping in the red-carpet room tonight." I replied, with fear in my voice.

Finding my boxed items in the dungeon, I gathered them and carried them over to the room with the red carpet. My breath escaped me while looking around the room. I hugged the boxes tightly in my arms, attempting to calm my terror-stricken nerves.

Carpet resembling a large square puddle of blood, flowed smoothly across the room. Matching in color, red paint had been splattered, and dabbed on the walls creating a messy bloody massacre vibe. With my parents going nuts about cleaning, painting, and redecorating, I must have missed them painting this room amid the commotion.

"Don't think about it. Just get your stuff moved in. It's gonna be fine." I mumbled to myself.

"I actually like it." Dad said entering the room carrying the head and foot boards to my bed. "I don't know where your mother got the idea of using an old feather duster as a paint brush, but it turned out looking pretty neat. Plus, it matches the carpet perfectly. I honestly thought the color of the paint was a shade darker."

"It is different." I mumbled depressingly.

Soon my bed was set up. The dresser, wardrobe, and other items I had here, were moved in. My old hickory wardrobe was tall, and fairly wide, taking up a large section of the blood splattered wall. A six-drawer red oak dresser helped blot out another smaller section. Having most of my stuff in here did make it a little less creepy I suppose.

"Shawn, supper is ready." Mom called from the kitchen.

I guess things were not as bad as they had seemed. Today had been a pretty good day for the most part. I had gotten to see a crazy man in the parking lot of the hardware store, picked my bedroom finally, which was the largest bedroom in the house, and it smelled like mom has cooked my favorite meal. Chili and grilled cheese. Not a bad day at all.

I stepped off of the red carpet, and onto the ugly green hallway.

'Dad really needs to do something about the poor lighting in the hall.' I thought to myself as the weak amber light flickered, faded, brightened somewhat, then dimmed again.

Passing underneath the indecisive light, it started happening again. Eerie footsteps sounding off right behind me.

'Echoes. Dad says it is only echoes.' I thought, slowing my stride. "Bare feet on sticky linoleum. That's all it is."

"Are you sure?" A woman's soft voice whispered in my ear faintly, proceeding to laugh hysterically sounding as though she were miles away while continuing to fade swiftly until no longer audible.

I tried to ignore it. I tried invoking my dad's way of thinking, we moved unexpectedly which was a life changing experience, thus my imagination was simply running rampant. That's all it was, nothing more. Proceeding once again to the kitchen, an echo of footsteps was no longer there in the grim hallway.

Taking my seat at the oval table, I filled my bowl full of mom's fantastic chili and crumbled some crackers over it. One cracker slipped from my grasp, and fell to the floor beside me. Reaching down to pick it up, I realized, the joke was on me. The voice, the laughter, instantly it all made sense. So much for dad's way of thinking. One tiny bit of assumption deteriorated his entire ideology.

"Shawn, are you ok? You are shaking something awful." Mom asked.

"Yeah, I just got a chill all of a sudden." I replied, while pondering how to continue.

I know what you're thinking, a chill? How lame is that? Yes, I am literally trembling with fear. What else am I to do? Do I make yet another frantic outburst informing them that we are, truly, not alone in this house? It hadn't worked any before. Mom and dad just dismissed everything. If only dad had witnessed mom and Marge glaring down the hallway, gazing into the dark oblivion like statues, and in a snap, or flick of the light switch, resumed their conversation as though the previous ten to fifteen minutes hadn't occurred. Maybe, just maybe, he could be more accepting of the reality we lived in now.

In an effort to verify that my dad's sticky floor-bare feet theory was nonsense, I gently lifted my foot off of the floor. …. No sound. I took another bite of the delicious chili and planted my foot down firmly on the floor. Again, I lifted it. No noise. No sound. Not flesh of a barefoot ripping away from the sticky linoleum. Why? What one aspect had dad not counted on??

Socks, I was wearing socks. Before, it had happened so suddenly I didn't have time to think about it. Now, now I was becoming a little less frightened of it all, almost numb to the happenings.

I began laughing, well more of an uncontrollable giggle. I was right for a change. Not that they would actually listen to reason, or anything. But I was nonetheless correct in my moment of epiphany. My giggles were a way I could celebrate without being told I was wrong, or that it was just water damage.

"Oh lord!" I blurted as tears from the laughter flowed down my cheeks.

"Son, what in the world has gotten into you?" Dad demanded.

"Stop that laughing with your mouth full before food gets sucked down your throat, and you choke!!"

Mom grunted loudly. Mom and dad both expressing silly looks of worry, concern, frustration, and total bewilderment fueled my laughing even further.

"I know you're not on drugs, are you son? When would you have had time? You've been with us all day." Dad bellowed angrily.

Mom flashed him a dirty look as he broke down and laughed with me. My teeth clamped shut, holding the chili in my mouth securely as to not, in fact, choke like mom insisted I would. Finally, losing breath, I gasped abruptly seeking more air in my lungs. One violent gasp sent a single chili bean hurdling toward my esophagus, and it got stuck at the top of my throat. I stood turning to face the trash can as fast as I possibly could, socked feet slipping and sliding on the puke green linoleum floor, causing me to nearly fall. Slipping still, what air had succeeded in finding my lungs, came rushing out. Partially chewed chili bits flew through the air with great force, plastering the inside and outside of our white trash can. One final cough sent the devilish chili bean flying out, striking the wall, then bouncing back and hitting me in the eye before ending its flight of destruction in the trash.

"I told you that would happen!!! You should've known better!!! Now get some napkins and clean that mess up right NOW!!!" Mom ordered.

"Ok, I will! I will." I say, having already retrieved napkins and some spray cleaner.

"What has gotten into you anyway? I for one would like to know instead of just joining in with my own chaotic laughing." Mom demanded, giving dad a stern look.

"I was just thinking about what dad had said about the sticky floor. I hadn't put any thought into it before, but the same thing happened just minutes ago. This time I was calmer, less freaked out, and eventually realized; I have socks on my feet. Kind of hard for socks, even if they stick to the linoleum, to make a noise loud enough to echo resembling additional footsteps. Just listen…." I say, sitting back down and lifting my foot over and over. Nothing, still no sound at all.

"Listen… my feet make no sound with my socks on. Same as the last time. I did have socks on when I first heard the other foot steps in the hall. The theory of it being an echo, has been disproven." I informed my parents with a big smile on my face, happy to be unarguably correct in my discovery.

"No, it hasn't. Look, you are sitting down for one thing. Not all of your body weight is on your feet right now, therefore it is not going to be as loud as if you were standing and walking. You are a big kid, so standing up, you will have a lot more weight on your feet. Just walk down the hall and back." Dad debated.

"I just wish we could drop all of this ghost nonsense. It's about to give me a migraine." Mom blurted.

Still thinking, knowing that I was on to something here, I happily got to my feet, and took a stroll down the hall. For the first time, I honestly did not hear extra footsteps. Turning at the doorway of my bedroom, I walked back. Instantly hearing footsteps that were not my own.

"See there, son? On your way down the hall you were stepping lightly, only to prove your point. On the way back, you were walking as you normally would, causing an echo. Sounding as if an extra person were walking. An echo is all it is, really." Dad smirked.

"I for one have had enough of this nonsense!! Shawn, get back here and finish eating, then go straight to bed. Tomorrow night, the first person to mention anything, even remotely suggesting a ghost, will find themselves in big trouble!!" Mom said angrily, glancing back and forth between my dad and myself.

I couldn't believe it. They still did not believe me. To make matters worse, I felt someone walking beside me as I walked back to the table. Or maybe I didn't. Maybe I couldn't believe me either. My thoughts, my senses, my emotions, mom and dad could be right. Perhaps I was simply having trouble adjusting to this new house.

6

Thin lacey red curtains, still showing creases from being folded in their packaging, failed to block out the magnificent sunlight now beating on my eyelids.

"What time is it?" I mumbled, awaking from sleep, and feeling as though I had just closed my eyes. My room had two windows, one beside my bed, and the other on an adjacent wall facing the back yard.

"It's almost 8:30 dear. Do you like these new curtains?" Mom asked, hanging more of them on the other window.

"Can we go to Brady's now?? Why is there so much red in my bedroom?? I hate it!!" I pleaded, pulling a pillow over my face to shield my eyes from the bright light filtering in the room.

"We will go after lunch. As for the red, I like it. When you get older and move out, you can decorate your house anyway you see fit. Until then, this may be your bedroom, but it is in my house. I will do whatever I want with it. By the way, breakfast is still on the table if you are hungry." Mom said sternly.

Blurry eyed, I made my way to the kitchen. I looked around, finding a bowl, a spoon, and breakfast cereal on the table.

"Some breakfast." I mumbled.

I ate, showered, and sat outside on the swing, patiently waiting for my parents to get ready to leave. The random noise of kids playing broke the silence. Looking over my shoulder, I saw several kids playing in water sprinklers at a house down the street. They appeared younger than me by several years, though one looked to be around my age.

Briefly, the boy near my age stopped running wildly through the sprinklers, and looked at me. He screamed loudly, then turned and tackled one of the other kids. I turned my attention back to the door. Watching, waiting, and hoping my mom and dad would step outside soon, all ready to go.

Two hours had passed before dad stepped out from around the corner of the house.

"Are you and mom ready to go yet?" I asked, longing to hear a pleasing answer.

"Go where Bub?" Dad replied, his face informing me of his confusion.

"We were supposed to go to Uncle George's today and see if Brady can sleep over tonight." I grunted.

"Oh yeah. I had forgotten all about that. Why don't you give them a call and see if they are even at home?" Dad suggested.

"Sure thing." I said grouchily. Sticking my thumb in my ear, and positioning my pinky at my mouth, I continued. "Hey Brady, what are you and Uncle George doing? Really, cool. Want to spend the night at my house tonight? That's great. We will be on our way to pick you up soon."

"You don't have to be so smart-alecky. The phone people, and the cable people, were both here earlier this morning. We have a phone, and television now. Go on in, pick up the phone and give Uncle George a real call." Dad snapped, failing to see an ounce of humor in my pretend phone conversation.

It was one joyous occasion to hear a dial tone again. A life time had passed by just waiting to hear that sound again. Being isolated from the entire outside world is nothing short of torment.

"Hello." Brady answered.

"Hey, what are you doing tonight? Wanna come over? Check out our new house? Spend the night? Hang out?" I rambled fast as though the call was about to be dropped.

"Whoa, I didn't catch half of that. Hang on and I'll ask dad what we are doing tonight…. (In the back ground) 'Dad! You awake?? Hey!! What are we doing tonight?? Shawn wants us to come over. …What? …Oh, ok.' …I'm back. The dictator said we have something to do today, but we will be there sometime tonight." Brady replied.

"…Cool. The sooner the better, though. We have a lot to talk about. I'm thinking about calling Mike and seeing if he can stay too. There are woods here, but don't know what, if anything at all, we could find. Might just have our adventure tomorrow." I replied with enthusiasm.

"I don't know if I can do that. My allergies have been going crazy the last couple of days. I'd probably just stay inside." Brady informed.

"Hmm, that stinks, but could be fun too. I haven't really even explored our new house much. It's a little on the creepy side. Actually, I haven't even been down to the basement yet. I can only imagine what it looks like." I remarked.

"What?? That would be the best part of moving into a new place. Getting to check everything out, digging through whatever the people that use to live there left behind. I bet you could find all kinds of cool stuff! Hey, when I get there, all I can say is finders' keepers." Brady said with a laugh.

"I honestly hadn't even thought of that. Mom and dad have been keeping me busy hauling trash out to be burned, and otherwise ransacking the place. I haven't even had a chance to look through what they are throwing away. There could be some cool stuff left behind…. I met the previous owners last night. They are some weirdos…Who knows, maybe they did leave something useful behind." I said with uncertainty.

"Well, like I said, if I were to find something cool, it's mine. How long have you all been there anyway?" Brady added.

"Just over a week now. Closing in on a week and a half." I stated.

"Cool. I'm gonna go, the dictator is hollering about something. I need to go see what he wants., but I will see ya later tonight." Brady assured.

Our conversation uplifted my soul a little. It would be nice to have a friend, or a cousin for that matter, here with me in this house of ghouls. I wanted to run and tell mom and dad the news. I was going to recommend that mom call and give Uncle George directions to our house later. I was a hundred percent certain he would need them with his misguided sense of direction. However, she and dad were running from one thing to the next, back and forth. So, instead, I just went outside and sat back down on the swing. It was a lot more peaceful out here, except for the kids yelling and screaming down the road.

A cool breeze stirred in the air, gently rocking the swing, sending me off into a pleasant nap. I saw it vividly in dream land, a glorious adventure with my friends. We wondered through the maze of woods, seeing joyful animals scurrying about, squirrels gathering nuts for their stock pile, rabbits bouncing happily along, deer and turkeys roaming freely. Bluffs, cliffs, and other interesting landscapes scattered abundantly throughout.

Suddenly, the sun light faded. Looking up to the sky, we could barely make out dark thunder clouds, swooping in beyond the close-knit tree tops. A hot day changed in an instant to a shivering cold as winter night. In the woods, we found ourselves without a light to brighten our path. We waited calmly for our sight to adjust to the darkness, but no adjustment came to assist us in this pitch-black environment.

Each of us stood, shoulder to shoulder, quietly, totally inert, and waiting. I knew if I broke, if I lost it now, being the very first one to do so would make me a wuss in that moment. I had to hang on, stay cool just a few more minutes, and wait on Brady or Mike to lose it first. Funny how these things work. I'm sure they were as scared and panicked as I, yet the first one to break always gets laughed at, becoming the catcher of an endless array of cry baby jokes. Eyes wide open, I saw nothing. I couldn't even tell where we were, where the nearest tree was, or even see the ground on which I stood. My heart raced, pounding loud enough to drown out all other sound.

'Whoa, wait a second. This is my dream? Why is it turning into a nightmare?' I thought, people can control their dreams, right? How had mine become so horribly derailed? Time to test that out, I'll just dream that something good happens, that someone slips in and saves us to all is well once again.'

"Hi boys!! …. I've been waiting on you!!" A creepy voice yells behind us, then trails off into a whisper, as psychotic laughter begins.

Without thinking, I turned and threw a punch. Pain rushed through my fist on impact.

"Ooooouch!!!" I yell. I opened my eyes and looked around with blurred vision. Grasping the knuckles of my left hand with my right hand, immense pain and stinging had my anger on a steady ascent. "What in the world did I hit? A brick wall?"

"No, you hit the back of the swing hard! I was sure those boards on the back were gonna break because they bowed way out!!" An unfamiliar voice said while laughing behind me.

I blinked my eyes a few times to clear my sight. I turned and saw the neighbor kid walking across our driveway.

"Did you say something else? Before that I mean? Something like you've been waiting or something?" I asked.

"No dude, I haven't said anything. I'm tired from running in the sprinklers all day. Thought I'd wait until I was closer cause I'm real tired, out of breath, and don't want to yell." Neighbor kid stated, huffing and puffing.

"Oh." I replied, getting annoyed by his laughter. I looked to the back of the swing. There, on the sharp edges of the boards constructing the back of the swing, were blood smears. Blood seeped out of two tiny cuts that were on my knuckles. "What do you want anyway?"

"Just thought I would walk up here and see if you wanted to hang out, maybe play some video games, ride bikes, or something. Do you like video games? Do you have any? What ya got? Huh? Huh?" He spoke quickly.

"I have an old game system. I got it about ten years ago. I've only got three or four games for it. My bike and four-wheeler haven't been moved over here yet. What is your name?" I asked.

"Cool, what are the games?" He blurted out.

"I have one hunting game, one racing, and one or two army type games." I answered.

"Cool, I like RPG's." He stated.

"Rocket Propelled Grenades?" I ask curiously.

"No ignoramus, role playing games. Have any of those? Do ya?" He asked.

"No, I don't think I do. Who are you again?" I asked once more.

"I'm Pete from down the street. Whatcha got to eat? Wanna play some games? It's hot out here, wanna go inside? Do you all have an air conditioner? Where did you move from??" He asked, speaking as fast, or possibly a little faster, than before.

"Nice to meet ya, Pete from down the street. I don't know, my mom should be fixing lunch anytime now. No, we don't have an A/C. We have always lived in this county, just a few miles away from here." I responded.

"That's just dumb. Why would you all move only a few miles away? If you are gonna move, move to another state or county, anyway. That would make more sense. What's for lunch? I'm hungry, haven't ate for a while. Why don't you have an air conditioner? Bet it's hot in your house, I might get dehydrated sitting in there." Pete rambled.

"Man, do you always talk that fast? I guess I listen slower than you talk, because I'm not catching half of what you are saying. Sure, we can go in and see if mom has started lunch yet. After that, I can try to find my games, if you want. Don't think I've seen them since the move, but I know I brought them." I replied dreading hanging out with Pete.

As we entered the kitchen, mom was on her way there from the other end of the long hall.

"Hey sweetie. Who's your friend?" Mom asked.

"Pete from down the street, he's tired hungry and wants to eat." I informed.

"That's not nice Shawn. Really you just met him, and are already making up stupid rhymes? I should ground you!!" Mom grunted, temper flaring.

"What? Seriously, he said his name is Pete, he lives in a house down the street, and the whole time he's been here he's been saying he want's something to …. devour? How's that? Is devour a better word to use?" I asked

"Hello new neighbor mom lady. I really am Pete from down the street. I've been playing with my cousins all day. I'm tired, hot, sweaty, and was outta breath. Now I'm hungry, craving anything, something to eat please." Pete rambled.

Mom took a step back, her eyes opened bigger than I had ever witnessed. She was completely taken aback by words being hurled toward her at the speed of light.

"Yeah, ok, I'll find you something to eat, ...Pete." She answered nervously.

Pete stood with a smirk on his face. Uncomfortable blue eyes glared at mom as she dug around in the refrigerator. Pete had sandy blonde, curly hair, slowly drying and becoming more poufy with each passing second. A couple years younger than me, a little heavier.

I took my seat at the table, enjoying the momentary peace, void of any word bombardment. It was hot today, really hot. Mom had all of the windows open, though the pleasant breeze outside seemed to navigate away from them. Tiny beads of sweat populated my forehead, and trickled down my face.

"Well boys, looks like I can fix you some sandwiches. I might have some chips too. I'm sorry I don't have much more than that. We've been too busy getting moved and everything, I haven't had time to get to the grocery store." Mom spoke, as she dug around in the fridge.

"Sounds good. I'll have a ham sandwich." I replied.

"I'll have the same, some chips, ...Do you have water? I want some ice water to drink. What about no bake cookies? They are great. Maybe an oatmeal pie? Ice cream, or something? I am pretty hungry. Haven't ate since breakfast. Why did you all only move a few miles away Ms. Neighbor mom? That doesn't make any sense. You all should really invest in an air conditioner. They are great. Or, maybe, just a big fan. I don't know. Any pets? I've got a dog. Our cat got ran over the other day. Must have been its last life because she didn't live through it. What do you do for a living? What's your name? My mom is Betty, and my dad is Roy. They are at work. They work all the time. When can we play your games? I'm the best, I'm really good as long as you don't cheat." Pete blurted.

And so, the rampage of words continued. Mom just looked at him in utter confusion as she placed our food and drinks on the table. She was not sure if she should answer, or attempt somewhat of a reply to words she may or may not have actually heard. Several long awkward milliseconds passed before she began inching away, then quickly walked to the back.

Somehow, the food sitting before him, had managed to push the continuing need for conversation out of his train of thought. He was an exceptionally noisy eater, a racket I was able to bare more than his border-line incoherent way of talking. His mouth operated at warp speed while chewing his food. Maybe it was a nerve issue he had, some weird disorder causing the motor skills in his mouth to function ten times faster than those of a normal person. Perhaps he was nervous since this was the first time, he had met us.

Shoving the last of his sandwich into his mouth, he took a long deep swallow. The kind of swallow that makes the croaking noise as your food slides down your throat. He turned up the glass of ice water, and sucked it down as if through a straw.

"So, where is your sister? That is your sister, isn't it? The girl I saw in the window earlier?" Pete asked seriously.

"I have a brother, no sisters. What window are you talking about?" I asked, surprised by how much slower his speech was. We were now having what resembled an almost normal conversation. I suppose his mouth working at full throttle had tired this odd kid out even more.

"I don't know. It was the window, I guess just past this one, by the sink. You really shouldn't lie, it's not nice. I can't lie. I get grounded when I do. My parents do not like liars at all." Pete replied in honesty.

"I am NOT a liar!! I have one brother named Joe. I have zero sisters!!" I said, a little upset at being called a liar.

"What? Are you ashamed of her or something? She looked kinda pretty. Long black hair, and a blue dress, I think. That's what it looked like she was wearing anyway." Pete stated, getting upset at my cluelessness.

He had seen her. … He was one odd kid, but he had seen the girl…I think. Upstairs she looked pitiful, far from pretty. He said the next window down, that would be the dungeon room.

"Let's go take a look if you are sure that is where you saw her. We will find out who she is since I have no sisters." I suggested.

We got up and exited the kitchen. Here we go, not knowing exactly what lay ahead. I acted big and brave, though I was not. I struggled with my jittery nerves, fighting to keep from shaking with fear as we walked down the grim hallway. My heart raced, praying for the room to be empty, totally vacant. I unintentionally paused for a moment, hesitating next to the doorway. My feet felt heavy, nearly bound to the floor, as though buried deep in dry concrete. I trembled all over, wondering what in the world made this seem like a good idea. I tried to lift my foot for another step, my leg failed to work. I felt like a broken robot, controls telling me to keep going, but extremities screaming malfunction.

"Are you chicken??" Pete asked.

My fear now pushed aside as a single bubble of anger rose up inside me. First a liar, now he called me a chicken.

"Come on." I mumbled, simultaneously stepping inside the dark room.

Everything appeared as it should be. Not one item out of place. The room still creepy as ever, but no sign of a girl in a blue dress. Breathing a sigh of relief, an icy cold mist poured down my body. The ambient air then returned to its normal high temperature.

"Well, where else would she be at? I'm sure she could've just walked to another room. It has been a little while since we were outside. Or maybe she ran away because you are too ashamed of her to admit you really do have a sister. ...A pretty one at that!" Pete bellowed.

"Hmm. There is only one other room on this side of the house. Doubt anyone would be in there." I said.

"Yeah whatever. I bet that is where she is hiding isn't it?" Pete asked, getting even more upset believing he was being lied to.

"I honestly don't know who, or what, you are talking about. But we can go check it out if you want. I'm up for finding out who the mystery woman is anyway." I stated, hoping to solve the mystery.

One room left, and simply the idea of it, had my stomach in knots already. I couldn't believe I was even going through with this investigation. I was wishing it would have ended at the dungeon. That the odd kid's curiosity would have been sustained at seeing the dungeon.

Slowly inching toward the wobbly, stretchy, bouncy room, strange noises filled the air. Noises one would only expect to hear at a butcher shop. My imagination got the best of me. In my mind, I pictured a large butcher knife chopping through flesh and bone. Limbs being tossed aside in some canister, gradually filling with blood. I went weak, trembling from head to toe. My head felt strange, as my muscles strained to keep my body upright.

"Man, our house is really hot today." I blurted. I got a sudden chill, running deep down inside me all the way to my skeleton. Droplets of sweat erupted all over me like a rash.

"Hey, do you feel ok?" Pete asked. "You are white as a sheet."

"Fine." I barely managed to reply. Now, leaning on the wall for support, I use to it to refrain from falling down, sliding my arm and shoulder along it to the very end of the hall. My eyes began to water steadily as we drew nearer to the doorway. A strange smell found its way into my nose, churning and wrenching my stomach. 'What is that stench?' I thought to myself. Noises continued, picking up speed, forming a strange rhythm as they went. Chop, shriek, shriek, splash, plop, chop, shriek, shriek, splash, plop, chop. The stench grew stronger and stronger causing my head to swim. Eyes watering so bad they could float right out of their sockets. Noise, smell, eyes burning....

<u>7</u>

"Shawn, seriously. Get up!" Mom yelled.

"Wha…" -I replied, in a whisper. My mouth was dry, tongue felt like sand paper. I tried to get some saliva in my mouth, but only a few drops formed. I rolled my tongue around for a bit, then repeated my question. "Wha, what? What is it mom?"

"I can't believe you! Aren't you old enough to know that if you feel sick, to go find a trash can or the commode? I had just finished painting that wall! Now look at it. It is completely ruined thanks to you, and I don't know if I have enough paint to fix it. You better pray that I do mister!" Mom raged.

Looking up at her, her face was a bright red color. I couldn't help but wonder how I had gotten down on the floor. I glanced into the bedroom with whacky walls, and saw vomit all over her freshly feather duster painted swatches. Bits of ham were plastered here and there, with a good dousing of dark soda. My stomach was still rolling insanely fast, and the smell…pierced my sinuses like a frosty icepick.

I closed my eyes for a moment, trying to find just an ounce of forgotten strength to get back on my feet. Arms still shaky as I rubbed my eyes. 'Where is Pete?' I thought to myself. I looked down the hall toward the kitchen, and found him standing at my feet. His face wore a blank expression, mouth hanging open, and for some reason, he was shirtless??

"Where is your shirt?" I blurted, weirded out by his lack of clothing.

"I gave it to your mom." Pete replied, sounding as confused as he looked.

"why did you give your shirt to my mom?" I asked.

"I don't know. I guess it seemed like a good thing to do." Pete answered, still looking dumbfounded.

"That sounds just as dumb as buying a house and moving into it, when it's only located a few miles away." I barked, still laying on the floor.

"…I don't think anything is that dumb. Are you ok? I was about to call you chicken again, but you collapsed before I could, and you hurled as you were falling. I didn't know if you had died or what happened to you." Pete stammered.

"Shawn, don't just lay there! Get up and help me try to clean this up, hopefully without messing up the paint. Come on Pete, from the street, wantin' to eat, you can help too." Mom ordered, as she came back from the bathroom with a hand full of old towels.

"He's Pete from down the street mom." I corrected.

"I don't want to eat now. I'm not hungry. Where is your daughter?" Pete replied.

"I don't have a daughter. I wouldn't even have time to take care of another child the way Shawn keeps me busy, Mr. Pete Street or whoever you are." Mom vented.

"So, you really don't have a sister?" Pete asked me quietly.

"No. I've already told you that a million times. Is it really that hard to believe?" -I replied quietly.

"I guess not, but it is hard to believe that you have a girl in your house, and you don't know who she is, or that she is in fact here. I know I saw a girl in the window." Pete said, continuing the conversation in hushed tones.

Extending his arm, Pete from down the street, helped me to my feet. I turned, looking into the vacant bedroom, now full of repulsive fumes including those of vomit.

"Mom, what is that smell? It's making me sick. I'm not trying to get out of helping clean my vomit, but it smells horrible in there." I asked from outside the doorway.

"Paint, paint thinner, and maybe some acetone. Probably a combination of all three." She replied.

"It all stinks then." I stated.

The strange room was full of a thick haze, composed of the fumes from everything she had mentioned. A square fan sat next to the window, failing to provide any adequate air circulation to rid the room of the dense, deadly vapors. To my surprise, an antique mirror, far beyond any logical use, was mounted on the wall facing the doorway. It was large, square in shape, with rounded corners, and held an exquisite, three-pronged top piece, with finely crafted swirled edges. It was hard to believe that it was an old mirror giving the room it's psychedelic appearance all along. Its silver backing had began separating from the glass, wrinkling and becoming spotted with mold, or mildew giving it a funhouse mirror effect.

'Aside from my suffocating brain cells, maybe this house isn't all bad.' I thought, as we delicately scrubbed the puke saturated wall. I realized in that moment, that my imagination needed some restraint instead of being free to run wild at will. Being terrified of getting sucked through a portal leading to another dimension, from merely walking into this room, had kept me away the entire time I've been here. Though, nothing is really special about this room, my fear obviously needs work.

As I was lightly scrubbing the last of the vomit off the wall and floor, mom returned from the bathroom.

"Here Shawn, it's your favorite color. This one is for you Pete Street, it's the only other one I have." Mom said, handing me an emerald green feather duster, and Pete a bright yellow one. "Get to work boys. Cleaning the throw up off of the wall took some of the paint off, or smeared what didn't come off completely. You two get to touch it up and make it look decent again."

"I didn't puke on the wall. Why do I have to repaint it?" Pete asked in utter confusion.

"Wrong place, wrong time Petey. Besides, with the two of you workin' on it, it shouldn't take very long to have it looking as good as before." Mom stated, then moved on to her next project.

"What a bummer. This is the last room I want to be stuck in." I mumbled.

"Yeah, well at least you aren't doing hard time for a crime you didn't commit!" Pete blurted.

"What are you talking about? Hard time? What crime?" I asked.

"Repainting this wall. I did not hurl on it, did I?" Pete stammered.

"Whatever. Mom isn't here, so I will fix it. How will she know anyway?" I said, and began dabbing the duster in light blue paint, then against the wall.

Time seemed to slow, while the fumes continued to rise. To make the smears less noticeable, I swirled the duster for better coverage of the blotchy areas. Finishing it up, I leaned back on my heels while kneeling to gain a broader scope of the wall. The wall almost looked it had when mom painted it.

"Not bad. Not bad at all." I said with the task complete.

"Cobwebs? You have a ton of cobwebs over by that old mirror!" Pete yelled, grabbing my arm tightly.

"What cobwebs? Mom has been cleaning in here and painting nonstop today." I replied, not seeing any cobwebs in the room. Pete gasped, and squeezed my arm tighter.

"Dan, I need you to come to our bedroom! Now Please." Mom screamed.

I turned to look at the mirror, but found no sign of the cobwebs Pete was freaking out about. He trembled, quivered and shook my arm, and whole right side in the process. I looked from the Mirror to Pete. Something black was on his chest and belly. All other color had escaped him, leaving him almost albino in contrast to the flat black liquid on him.

Pete started making a strange indescribable noise, unlike any I had heard before. His eyes locked on something deep inside the mirror. His mouth hung open, lips jiggling as the weird sound flowed steadily from his vocals. A noise sounding like his lungs were blocked, like his voice box was ready to spit out another slew of incoherent ramblings, but the air supply just wasn't there.

"Dan, hurry up! I am so sick of this, I could Scream." Mom yelled at dad again.

"I'm coming dear, just a second!" Dad yelled in response.

Pete, was frozen stiff, shaking frantically, and squeezing the life out of my arm. Blackness now crept along his forehead. I turned to look at the mirror again, to try and figure out what was wrong with him.

"How did that happen?" Dad asked curiously.

"Shawn, get in here this instant! Did you do this? If you did, you are ground for the rest of the summer!" Mom yelled.

"I haven't done anything mom!" I yelled back, turning my head to face the hall instead of the mirror. "I think something is wrong with Pete!! You should come and see what you think is wrong with him!"

As those words left my lips, my attention returned fully to the mirror.

"God… God… OOOOHHH GOOOOOOOODD!" I screamed. My vocals were in no way restrained to hush my hysterical screams. Wasting no time, I was on my feet, grabbing Pete's arm, and running full speed toward the living room door.

Pete managed to find his speech once again, when he no longer had the mirror in sight. Screaming at the top of our lungs, we raced down the ugly green hall, and blasted past mom and dad's bedroom door. Dad yelled something as we fled, inaudible due to mine and Pete's yelling. Reaching for the handle on the screen door, eye's looking outside for safety, I missed the handle. With Pete hot on my trail, I collided with the door, then Pete crashed into me knocking the door open, and we tumbled out onto the deck.

"What in the world do you two think you are doing? What did you do to Pete? You two almost tore the door off of the hinges!" Dad grunted standing in the door way.

"Sorry, sorry, sorry, I'm sorry. I'm not going back in there ever again. Never. Don't ask. It's not happening. I want to go home!!" I cried.

Pete on his back beside me, propped himself up on an elbow, and looked at my dad. The only sound escaping his lips was a hissing sound.

"Hey, are you ok? What were you two boys doing? What were you thinking stampeding down the hallway like that? Well, answer me for crying out loud." Dad demanded.

I don't know what Pete had actually seen in the old mirror, but I had a hunch. When I looked back at the mirror the last time… I couldn't believe my eyes. "Not saFe!! No oNE CaN hElP!!! He'S waTCHhing!!! GeT oUt WhILe YOu cAn!!!!" Was scribbled backwards all over the walls in a flat black paint. Looking into the mirror the last time, I saw the words on the wall. Their reflections in the mirror made them easily readable. The letters were still wet, with paint rolling down the walls from an excessive amount being used.

Several minutes passed, Pete was still hissing like an angry snake. I was too scared and baffled to say anything. Dad walked from the doorway, and took a leaning stance on the railing. Heavy footsteps came stomping down the hall, through the living room, then mom slung the screen door open.

"Is that your idea of a joke? Did you do that Pete? You didn't seem very happy about having to help Shawn fix the paint on the wall. Was it you? Or was it both of you just doing it to make me angry?" Mom bellowed, her temper quickly building pressure.

Pete threw his left arm over his stomach, index finger pointing to me.

"SSSSS. SSSSS. SSS, hiss sister!!! SISTER, HIS SISSTER DID IT!!! She was in the .... she was in the mirror! I saw her again. She was in the mirror. Her black hair was flowing out of the mirror, but she was in the mirror. His sister was in the mirror and writing on me." Pete stuttered finally.

"Pete, I think you should go home now. Shawn doesn't have a sister. I'm the only woman in this house for that matter. Just tell me honestly, was it all you or did Shawn help?" Mom inquired.

"It was the girl in the mirror. His sister." Pete said, panting for air.

"Fine, have it your way. Don't be surprised when you find out that I have called and told your parents about everything!" Mom stated, raising her voice.

Pete got to his feet. He looked from me, to mom, then back at me. The look on his face, let us all know, his mind was lost. The simple world he had known for so long, had just been turned upside down. "ViCTim" written on his forehead, "ParEntS can'T save YoU" scribbled on his chest and belly. Clearly, warnings of something terrible yet to come. Maybe mom and dad will realize it, and move us back home and away from here…or farther away from here than we were.

Taking notice that his welcome had been worn out, Pete headed back to his home down the street. Still shirtless, and running in a silly manner. He looked odd with his arms grasping thin air in front of him to help propel him at top speed, almost as if he were swimming. He glanced every few seconds over his shoulder to look at our house with his scared blue eyes.

Thrust into the air, and back on my feet like a rag doll, dad's grip on my arm was one I couldn't slip out of.

"Come on young man. First you have some explaining to do starting with our bedroom door. Then, I want to know what happened, and what is so terrible about the room you boys were in!" Dad said angrily.

My head bobbled lifelessly on my shoulders as I was led through the living room, kitchen, and down the hall. How could I explain something I knew nothing about? What would it take to get them to see things as they were, and not as they imagined them to be? This was by far starting out to be the worst summer break ever.

"Let's hear it! Why did you do this? Better yet, just what did you do exactly, anyway? This is a brand-new door!!" Dad demanded in urgency.

"Looks like more water damage. When is the roof being repaired?" I pointed out.

"That is what it looks like, but that doesn't answer any of my questions. This is a metal door, and should not be like this. The other door was a wood panel door. The water had the panel crinkled, bowed out from typical water damage to a wooden door. Metal will rust, not do the same thing. So, what exactly did you do to it?" Dad demanded.

"I have no answer for ya. I haven't even been in here aside from waking up in here, and when we put this door up. Maybe it is just some sort of defect with the door itself." I replied.

"Maybe. I'm going to call the building supply store and see if they have received any other complaints such as this. Come on, next room." Dad said, jerking me into the hallway. "Why in the world did you boys do this? What is that stuff anyway? Magic marker? Paint? Where did you get black paint at? I haven't got any, haven't seen any around here either." Dad thundered.

All four walls bore warnings. Some of the words were backwards on the walls but, easily legible while looking in the dismal old mirror. More of the same had been written after Pete and I ran out of the house, only written normal instead of backwards. Same words, over and over again, had been painted all over the walls, leaving little trace of the blue painted by dusters. I couldn't believe how quickly the words had appeared. From Pete's reaction to the mirror, he must have seen the gruesome dead girl or woman that I had encountered upstairs. It didn't make any sense, though. The first time Pete saw her, he thought she was pretty. Maybe he just didn't get a good look at her. To make matters worse, apparently now someone else, a "he", is watching me? Pete? Us? It would be nice if the warnings were a little more specific, and less cryptic.

"So, what happened in here? What exactly made this seem like a good idea? Was it the other kid? Did he do this?" Dad asked, his face red with anger.

"Dad, all I know is we were in here. I was touching up the paint for mom, then all at once Pete started acting strange. Mom yelled for you, then called for me. I looked at Pete, he was scared stiff, and when I looked at the mirror, I saw all of this written on the walls. I don't know how it happened. Maybe we should get the weird old couple back to answer these questions. Other than that, I don't have any answers." I stated.

"I hope you like it in here. Here is some white paint and a roller. You get to paint this room all over again, as soon as that mess dries." Mom said, dropping a gallon of white paint and a paint roller on the floor by my feet.

"Fine. But one of you has to stay in here with me while I paint. I am not going to be in here by myself!" I pleaded.

"Hey. How are you? Wow… What happened in here?" Joe asked peeking through the door.

"Your little brother, and some kid from down the street did this. I don't know where they got the black paint. I know we don't have any here." Dad reported.

"Yeah, this makes twice he gets to paint in here. He puked on that wall earlier, and messed it all up." Mom added.

"Is the kid down the street pretty tall? I don't think Bub can reach all the way up to the ceiling in here. Not unless he was on a step ladder or something." Joe noticed.

Finally, someone talking with some sense. Someone questioning this ordeal for a change, instead of simply casting blame on me. Hopefully Joe could make them see what was really going on here.

"I don't know how they did it. The other kid is shorter than Shawn. Still, those two were in here when it happened, so it's pretty obvious who did the crime." Dad replied coldly.

"Still seems a little strange. Bub, why did you two do all of this? Mom and dad work hard, and this is downright disrespectful." Joe demanded.

"Joe, all I know is that we were in here, I was touching up this wall one minute, then bam! All of these words were here." I stated in all honesty.

"Likely story Bub. Looks like you have your work cut out for you tomorrow. Anyway, mom, dad, pretty nice-looking house here." Joe complimented.

"Thanks, we have done a ton of work so far. Come on. I'll give you the tour, then you can go outside

with your dad and he can show you around out there."
Mom invited.

As the three of them vacated the room, I had no intention of hanging around by my lonesome. I hurried out, and onto the deck, taking a seat on the swing. So much for the idea of Joe being a voice of reason. The noise of kids playing down the street no longer plagued the air. The sun was setting, fading just beyond the tree tops. I looked down the street, almost hoping to see Pete walking back up to my house. Sadly, he was not. This day was coming to an end, slipping by me with the greatest of ease. I had forgotten all about calling Mike, and having mom to Call Uncle George to give him directions. What a day indeed, leaving me to realize just how helpless one can be amid things no one wants to believe, or attempt to understand. A tear rolled from my eye, down to the tip of my nose, and dropped through the cracks of the swing as I fell asleep.

"Son, are you going to wake up?" Dad asked, shaking me gently.

"What? …No… I don't know." I mumbled in response.

"Bub, Brady is here. Him and uncle George came to visit. You should wake up for a while and socialize. Then you can go back to sleep when they leave." Joe added.

"Joe? Why are you still here?" I asked, surprised Joe was still there. Usually he was always in a hurry, unless it was a weekend that he wasn't working.

"I was about to leave, but they showed up and we've been talking. Been trying to wake you up for almost an hour." Joe explained.

Looking around, they were all talking about usual stuff. Fun times back when they were kids, each with a tall tale of their own. Even Joe had a few tales to make us laugh. I was on the sofa, Joe, or maybe dad, must have carried me inside and laid me down there. Mom had the windows opened allowing the surprisingly cold night air to flow freely throughout our house. Where was that kind of circulation when we needed it earlier today?

"Hey Brady. Want to go see my room?" I asked, wiping slobber from my chin.

"Yeah, sure. I brought some new comics over. You can check out. We can leave the AD-ults to their dumb stories and hang out in your room." Brady joked.

When we got to my room, I uncontrollably blurted out everything. A nonstop, full speed rant, about the house, the ghost, the writing, the kid down the street, every minor detail. Brady listened intently, as if he were collecting data. I could see it in his eyes, with each statement I rambled off, a chart was slowly taking shape somewhere in his mind. Lists were being made, processed, referenced and cross referenced, as fast as the data was being collected. Having a book nerd as a friend, a cousin even, could be a good thing.

By the time I had finished my rant, I was out of breath, falling over on my bed. Talking fast, taking short breaths, just to continue my speech had left me feeling light headed.

A long silent pause ensued. At this point, not much of anything would be surprising to me. If Brady were to respond with 'Ok, how about saying all of that again, but in slow-motion.' I wouldn't have expected less. Instead he sat on the edge of my bed, newest comics in hand, looking at me. I just knew something was brewing in his mind. Some wheels were turning, digging for a semblance of logic. Eagerly, I waited for his response.

"I have to ask, kind of a dumb question at this point really. Do you feel that? It just feels like we are being watched. Like someone is close by, close enough to be looking right at us, yet off away from us somehow." Brady asked.

"I don't know. Maybe. It could make sense given the state of things. I haven't exactly had that feeling the time we've been in this house." I replied, getting cold chills.

"For some reason, I've felt that. The whole being watched feeling. It started the second we pulled into your driveway." Brady stated, almost happily.

"That is odd. It's never seemed like I was being watched. Only random things happening. Even when I was upstairs, I didn't feel that. Then again, she would have been facing away from me because I could hear the rope twisting, then she leaned out into the light, and turned to face me." I stated.

"Well, I didn't notice your 'sister' in the window, or anything when we got here. Still, I've been getting cold chills because of it, off and on. I did read in a book one time, that the worst thing to do is try to contact a ghost or spirit. Basically, it said if you do that, then everything will get worse. Kinda open the doorway for it to cross over into our world. Good thing Mike isn't here. He would be trying to talk to this mystery girl or woman." Brady joked.

"So, what am I supposed to do? Ignore it and hope it goes away? If these weird occurrences keep happening, my parents…I really don't know what they will do. They are one hundred percent certain that either me, Pete from down the street, or both, wrote all of that in the other room. As of now, you are the only one who believes me. Joe questioned it a little, but he just brushed it off like mom and dad, accepting that it was mine or Pete's doings." I grunted.

"Joe is cool. I would've guessed he would have investigated further before blaming you." Brady replied.

"So did I. But he just sided with them, and then mom gave him a tour of this stupid ghost house. Yeah, I guess it depends on which version of her that Mike saw. Pete said she was pretty. The girl I saw was repulsive, a dead rotting corpse with bare bones showing in most areas of her face and hands. There were bits of flesh still hanging on for dear life, dangling here and there." I elaborated.

"If I know Mike, that would probably only peak his interest. Doubt it would matter at all to him. I have read a few books where the ghost or spirit was in need of something, some form of help before they could move on. If that is the case, then acknowledging it might work out ok. It just depends on the ghost." Brady laughed, knowing my response.

"Well, that's nice. Still not much help. How am I supposed to know which to do? Do I ignore it, or do I try to have a conversation with her?" I asked.

"That is a good question. Has it tried to hurt you, or to really mess anything up?" Brady inquired.

"Just when it tried to grab me upstairs, and yeah the room is a disaster. Mom and dad's bedroom door had 'water damage', so we got a new door, and put it up yesterday. Today, the new metal door has 'water damage'. To answer your question, yeah, she has done stuff. Has she been successful in hurting anyone or anything? …not really, other than messing up the paint." I clarified.

"I don't know what to tell ya man. If she's mad or disgruntled, and knowing already that she can get to you, it could be a bad idea trying to talk to her. Did you talk to Mike today?" Brady spoke, still seeking a method of resolve in his mind.

"Why me? Why do I have to deal with this? No, I was going to call him, but then the neighbor kid came up and I forgot all about it. Are you staying tonight, or do you have to go back home?" I pondered.

"I'm not sure, Captain Dictator didn't really say one way or the other. I'll ask him again in a few. I have never seen a ghost, or anything weird like that before. It would be cool to stay and hopefully see something crazy happen." Brady replied, looking forward to a chance encounter.

"Sure, it's easy for you to say. You won't be the one getting in trouble." I stated.

"Hey I don't care. It would be worth it. I would happily take the blame just for the chance to witness writing magically appearing, or a ghost whispering in my ear as I walk through the house." Brady said with a laugh.

"Fine. Let's go ask your dad. Maybe you will get to see something. If you're gonna take the blame, it will get mom and dad off of my case. That is, if they believe that it was you who messed something up." I grunted.

Walking into the living room, the grownup's conversation was still lively. Moving from one to the next, taking turns telling tall tales to the others. Most of the tales were logical, believable. A few sounded like they were fluffed a little too much, to be more entertaining.

"Dad?" Brady beckoned as mom wrapped up a tale of her own.

"Oh me. What is it son?" Uncle George answered, still laughing at a story my dad had told.

"Care if I spend the night with Shawn tonight?" Brady asked.

"Oh, I don't know. I don't know what we are going to be doing tomorrow." Uncle George replied.

"Probably the same thing we did today, not much of anything. Whatever you dream up for us to do tomorrow, I will work three times as hard the day after to get it done, along with anything else you have planned." Brady bargained.

"Sounds like he wants to stay pretty bad to make a deal like that." Joe stated.

"I'll have to think about that. After the day Shawn has had, I don't know if he deserves to have a friend sleep over. What do you think Cheryl?" Dad added, to the dilemma.

"You all might as well let him stay. It might do Shawn some good. After they fix that room, maybe they can run around here, and Shawn can get a little more used to the place. It seems to me like he's having trouble adjusting to the change, and it could help him more than anything." Joe suggested.

"I hate to say it, but Joe might be right." Mom agreed.

"I guess you can stay. You better not do anything to mess their house up, or any other kind of mischief." Uncle George decided.

"Thanks everyone. I owe you all one." I replied gratefully.

"Well people, I'm gonna have to get home. I have to be at work early tomorrow. If you all need anything just give me a call." Joe said, getting up and walking outside.

"Just don't forget it either Shawn. You can start paying me and your father back by repainting that room tomorrow." Mom said coldly.

Brady and I turned to go back to my bedroom, and devise a strategy against the ghost girl or woman. Joe, quickly and quietly ran back inside.

"Dad, I just saw some man walk into your barn!" Joe informed dad in hushed tones.

Dad got up, hurrying as quietly as possible to his bedroom, and grabbed his .38 special revolver. Brady and I stood in the hall, with our backs against the wall as not to be in the way. When dad stepped back into the living room, Uncle George and Joe followed closely behind him outside, and around the corner of the house toward the barn. Mom went out on the deck, standing at the corner of the house, and peeking around to see what was going on.

"Shh, go back inside!!" Mom whispered as me and Brady stepped out.

"No way am I going to be left alone in there." I whispered back.

We walked up behind mom, and stood in the silence. My heart raced, guess Brady's unshakable feeling of being watched was real. I wonder if it was the man that the ghost was warning us about? I knew deep down, if someone or something was there, dwelling inside dad's barn, they would find him. I expected at any moment to hear one of them yelling back, instructing mom to call the police. I tried to listen, hoping to hear something of significance to shed light on what was happening. Loud thumps from my racing heart drowned out any faint sound, or noise. Brady stood beside me, looking like all was well, with a goofy look on his face. Dad with a gun, my brother and Uncle all together, possibly chasing someone in the darkest hours of the night without a flashlight, had my nerves on edge.

"You ok?" I whispered to Brady, wondering why he appeared as though nothing were happening.

"Yeah, I'm fine. Whoever is in your barn should worry though. Those three lunatics going in after him, and having a gun. Oh yeah, that guy should be worried." Brady replied, in a normal tone, a smile spreading across his face.

"That is true." I replied, trying to smother a cackle.

Mom eased around the corner of the house. I moved closer, and peeked around. I couldn't see anything in the darkness. A few seconds later, my eyes had adjusted some. I think, maybe, it looked like…no... I still couldn't see anything. I moved back, placing my back firmly on the front of the house, and listened to the silence filling the air.

Several minutes passed, still clueless about what was happening in our back yard. Brady slid down the wall taking a seat on the deck. I turned slowly to try and see something, anything, in the back yard. Straining my eyes in the darkness, three bright flashes of light ripped through the air followed by explosions.

"Oh no! I hope dad didn't shoot whoever that was in our barn. He will go to prison! Oh man! Oh man! No!" -I stammered.

"I seriously doubt he has shot anyone. If he did, then it was probably self-defense. Calm down!" Brady said.

We sat there on the deck. Light from the living room being cast out of the window, gently grazing the tops of our heads, and tips of our toes on the deck. It felt like an eternity had passed when the four of them returned.

"I don't know where he would have gone. But someone was in my barn. Both of the doors were open, and some of our gardening tools were tossed out behind the barn. Wish I knew who it was. I'd call Sherriff Tom, and have him go pick the fella up and haul him to jail. A thief is the only thing I hate. No one else is as worthless as a thief." Dad mumbled, through gritted teeth.

"Was something stolen?" I asked

"Yeah, whoever it was made off with dad's chain saw, and a saddle." Joe reported.

"Looked like he was gonna make off with your shovels, rakes, and hoes, the way he had them bundled up." Uncle George added.

"Did you put a lock on the barn doors? What if he comes back?" Mom asked.

"I'll have to run to town in the morning, and get a couple locks and some chain. Tonight, I will be keeping an eye on it. Kinda hope he does come back in a way. If he does, I might figure out where my chainsaw and saddle went." Dad said, his face a deep red as they stepped up on the deck.

"Poor fella. He must not know you all very well. You're the last man I would want to be mad at me." Brady joked.

Dad flashed Brady a look of accomplishment, then proceeded inside.

"Boys, it's late, and you all need to get some sleep. Where are you two sleeping at?" Mom inquired.

"Well, I'm sleeping in my bed. I don't know about Brady." I replied.

"I'll just sleep on the floor in Shawn's room, if that's ok?" Brady replied.

"That's fine. I'll grab a blanket and a pillow for you to sleep on." Mom stated, going into her room.

Almost as soon as my head touched my pillow, I was out. Powerless to resist as the cool night air flowed gracefully through my open window, and across my bed. When my eyes closed, I was no longer one with this reality. I spiraled down, out of control into the darkness. Falling faster, faster, and faster toward dream land. I just hoped any dream this night was more pleasant than the last.

"Hey Shawn. Shawn." Brady called to me.

"What?" I answered, trying to open my eyes.

"What is going on? Is this some kind of dream?" Brady asked.

"I don't know. I don't care. I'm tired. Let's just go back to sleep. Or not. I don't know." I mumbled, somewhere in the foggy area between sleep and wakefulness.

"I don't think this is a dream. I mean, why would both of us be in the same dream? The same exact dream taking place in your bedroom. I can't move. Can you?" Brady continued.

"Yeah sure. Dream, room, no move, both of us. Whatever." I mumbled.

"Hey, I'm serious. I'm like paralyzed or something. Are you? Or can you actually move more than just your mouth?" Brady persisted.

"I don't know. Can you open your eyes? I don't think I can." I asked, beginning to realize what Brady was talking about.

"No. ...Do you hear that?" Brady shrieked.

"Yeah, what is it? Sirens? Police?" I asked.

"I think so." Brady replied.

Laying in my bed, my body was lifeless. I felt nothing. My eyes were locked shut. I struggled, using all of my effort to try to lift a single eyelid, to no avail. I could talk, I could hear, and I could smell. My neck, I could move my neck a little. I frantically twisted my head from side to side, trying to get some feeling back into the rest of me. With each twist, my head seemed to slowly build some momentum. Feeling came and went just as quickly.

Supersonic flashes of blue light beat on my eyelids. A lurid siren screeched wildly, terrorizing my ear drums. Panicked, I kept slinging my head side to side as hard as I possibly could. The siren grew louder, in time with the speed of the blue light, both increasing steadily. I tried to scream, scream for my parents to save us, but it was as if my vocal chords were dead. Either that, or I was unable to scream louder than the screeching siren. Couldn't my parents hear this? Why hadn't it woken them up?

"I think my ears are bleeding!" Brady yelled.

I tried to yell back, to let him know mine were too, but I had no voice. My mouth, my voice, neither of them would cooperate with me. At least I could still turn my head, and did so as though my life depended on it. Back and forth, back and forth. As violently as I could manage.

Finally, with my neck hurting, burning, and possibly even ready to snap, I rolled onto my side. I turned my head one last time, chin directly above my shoulder. When my body started to fall onto my stomach, I quickly shoved my head down on the corner of my pillow. After my body crashed to the mattress, my face slid down my pillow, forcing my right eye open. Vibrant blue streaks of light erupted into my bedroom from outside my windows. The sirens had grown so high pitched, I could no longer hear them, only deafening ringing in my ears. I rolled my eye to see Brady. I found him on his back on the floor, at the foot of my bed, his mouth opened wide. I guess he was screaming bloody murder at the top of his lungs, but I heard nothing aside for the horrid ringing.

The blue light continued, flashing faster and faster. Eventually, my room was illuminated by the brilliant blue hue. I suppose it was still flashing, only far too fast to be noticeable now. My one eyelid, held open by my pillow, slipped and fell shut. I could still see the bright blue light through my closed eye lids.

"I'm still trying to figure this out. Being a ghost, I mean. Sorry for the light show, but this is the best I can do. Promise you won't scream for help, and I will release my hold on you two." A girl's voice spoke. Her vocals bouncing and echoing down a warped distorted hallway.

"I promise. Please stop this now." Brady begged.

"I promise, but only if you tell me why you are doing this." I replied.

Instantaneously, I could move again. My arms, legs, fingers, toes, all functioning as they should. I sat up on my bed, looking at Brady on the floor. He sat up, looked at me, then we turned our attention to the corner of my bedroom. There she stood. Flickering like a light about to blink out of existence. A dreaded stench escaped her, filling the air. In the blinking light, she was changing from the old decaying rotten corpse ghost I had encountered upstairs, to appearing normal and beautiful. Or pretty as Pete had referred to her. Each flicker presented a rotation of the two versions. Clothed in the midnight blue dress with white polka dots, her hair levitated in the air, like it was charged by static electricity in both visions we saw. Is this the end? Were we done for? Was she going to wreak havoc on us at any moment?

Anticipation grew, as did my fear. Too afraid to move, too afraid to speak, I was imagining the worst possible outcome for Brady and myself. How does one fight a ghost? A girl ghost at that? It's not right for a guy to hit a girl. Being a girl, and a ghost, I still didn't think it would be right. I wouldn't even want to hit her with all of the maggots pouring from the rotten version of her. How gross would that be? Punch her only to have maggots fly everywhere?

"What happened to you? Why are you tormenting me? Who are you?" I asked angrily.

"I'm Susan. My parents, Marge and Lloyd think they killed me. I thought so too at first. I found out that it wasn't them. Some... thing, I guess, I'm not exactly sure what he or it was. He used my parents like they were puppets, making them do what they did to me." Susan spoke, her voice still warped and sounding like an echo. The whole time rising in volume, then falling and fading out.

"What did they do?" Brady asked intently.

"He made them put that noose around my neck. Lloyd pulled it tight over the top of my bedroom door, hoisting me off of the floor. He made Marge shut the door securing the rope in place. Lloyd pulled harder and harder on the rope, strangling me, breaking my neck. Blood flowed from the back of my neck after my broken spine tore through, soaking into the rope, and leaking all over the inside of the door. With my life extinguished, mom and dad were of no further use to him. He disappeared into the woods. When they realized what they had done, mom still holding the door closed, dad with the rope wrapped around his hands, they went a little nutty." Susan continued, beginning to weep.

"There's your water damage." Brady chuckled.

"So, what are you saying? That, man or thing is after me now?" I asked.

A tear rolled down the cheek of the lively version of her, a maggot slid down the cheek of the rotten one.

"Yes. Though, I think I can help. I want my revenge for what he did to me. You have to help me though. Somehow, he can roam freely, yet I'm confined to this place. I need you to lure him out of the woods. I should be able to take care of the rest." Susan declared.

Brady and I looked at each other. Thoughts raced through my mind. I didn't know if we should trust her or not. Brady's facial expression suggested he thought the same.

"If we help you, will this be the end of everything? I mean will you stop bothering me and my family?" I asked.

"Yes. I was only trying to get your attention. I never meant to scare you, or cause you any dismay.

Time is of the essence, and it is really running out. I don't want your fate to be that of my own." Susan insisted.

"Ok, we will help. Our mission will commence around noon tomorrow. But you better be ready Susan." Brady agreed.

"Noon?" I asked, wondering why noon.

"Yeah. Hopefully we can have that room fixed, eat lunch, and be ready for your woodland exploration adventure. How will we know when we find him? Is he just a man?" Brady replied cheerfully.

"You will know it when you find him. You just will. Sometimes he is a man, looking crazy and homeless, with a badly scarred bald head. Sometimes, he has no real physical appearance. Maybe only an odor, change in temperature, a mist, or a cool breeze. But you will know, without a doubt, when you have found him." Susan attempted a description.

"Ok," I replied. The ghost of Susan blinked, flickered, and was gone. A third person would be ideal for this, but I had forgotten to call Mike earlier. It would have been nice to have a tough guy with us for this task.

Sleep evaded me the rest of the night. I lay in bed with my eyes closed wanting to fall asleep. I wanted to forget about everything, wake up and say to Brady 'man I had the strangest dream last night.' That's all I wanted it to be anyway, a dream. A crazy ghost girl wanting me and Brady to wander off into the woods and find some man ghost thing that we might not even be able to see. This was insane. Oh yeah, we will just know it's him when we find him, even though we may not be able to see him. That is by far the most absurd thing I had ever heard in my life. …or it would have been if we hadn't moved.

Brady seemed a little too eager, but he probably had some idea of how this would all play out. He owns hundreds of comic books about supernatural beyond the grave type events. Why couldn't this all just have happened to him instead? Not wishing him misfortune, but he was more suited for all of this paranormal stuff. What about me? The horror film extraordinaire? After encountering a real-life ghost, I didn't care if I never saw another horror flick again. The sad reality of it all, was that even in fiction, there was an ounce of fact.

Lost in my thoughts, I could hear mom and dad's alarm going off in the next room. This was one day I absolutely did not want to get started. Bad thing was, I couldn't play sick, or possum, and get out of it. Mom was dead set on us painting that room again today. Even with Brady being here, I was still worried. What if we managed to lure that thing out of the woods, but he tore us to shreds before Susan could help? My stomach was in knots thinking about how bloody we were going to die today.

"Rise and shine boys! Let's eat some breakfast, and get to work! Come on, get up you two!" Mom beckoned.

"I'm awake." Brady answered. "Shawn, you awake?"

"I don't want to be. But yeah. I couldn't go back to sleep." I respond, after some hesitation.

"Me either. I had a weird dream last night. On a good note, I think I have a plan." Brady mumbled.

"I don't think it was a dream, Brady. It really happened. Do you think she was telling the truth?" I replied, unexcited about our 'mission' as he called it.

"Oh that. I know that wasn't a dream. That was way too weird. I had a dream before that all happened." Brady stated.

"I don't like the idea of being bait for some …whatever it is we are after." I grunted.

"Yeah, when you think of it that way it doesn't sound like a good time. Anyway, I've got this. I actually think we can handle it." Brady said enthusiastically.

We ate breakfast in a hurry. Mom kept rushing us, and reminding us of what the day had in store for us. I dreaded it all. Mom finished eating a few minutes before Brady and myself. She was getting all the paint supplies together, cleaned, mixed, and ready to go for us. My neck ached, stiff as a board from the thrashing last night. Brady did not seem himself at all. That made me paranoid about him possibly being a puppet, helpless to do the chaotic bidding of the …thingamajig.

Entering the room, it was far gloomier than before. The flat black words scribbled everywhere, made it darker than ever, maybe even darker than the dungeon. Repeatedly I found myself glaring into the antique mirror, and wondering what it was that Pete had seen in there. Looking at it now, close up, I only saw crinkled foil, mildew, and corroded grayish green splotches.

My nerves were on edge, I was expecting at any minute to see the…entity Susan described come floating out of the mirror, or in through the door. Who knew, Susan herself might make another appearance. That would be wonderful. I couldn't imagine how much more trouble I would be in if those words were to magically reappear. Even with mom in here helping us, I'm sure the blame would still fall on me.

"Good job guys. It looks really good. I will go fix you all some lunch. We will let it dry for a few hours, and then we will go over it again with the feather dusters." Mom complimented.

"Feather dusters?" Brady asked, sounding confused.

"Yeah, haven't you noticed every other room here other than the dungeon? Mom has gone crazy painting with feather dusters now. She saw it on one of those 'Do It Yourself' shows on T.V. They have all been paint dusted!" I joked. "Hey Brady, do you smell that odor? Do you think it's the thingamajig?"

"I get it. I was wondering how you all got the paint to look the way it did in the other rooms. That stinks! Man, you must have more gas than the gas companies!" Brady laughed, pinching his nose. "Let's eat really fast, then head to the woods. I can't wait, but I hope my allergies don't flare up again like they have the past few days."

"Glad one of us is excited." I replied.

While we were sitting at the table, mom fixed grilled cheese and gave us some 'sour cream & onion' chips. I took a small bite of a grilled cheese. Cheese squirted into my mouth, thick, gooey, and HOT!!! I chugged half a glass of strawberry soda to cool my scorched tongue. Brady laughed at me as he swallowed the last of his chips. He gave eating fast a whole new meaning.

"Wasn't your grilled cheese hot?" I asked.

"It was, but it was really good. If I wasn't full, I could probably eat another one." Brady said smiling, eager to get our 'mission' started.

"Want mine?" I offered.

"No, I said I'm full. I'm going outside. Come on out as soon as you get done." Brady insisted.

I tried to hurry and finish my food. Well, maybe not hurry to fast or anything. I wasn't going to swallow it all in four bites as he had. After I finished, I went out on the deck. To my surprise, immediately, I heard the nervous ramblings of Pete from down the street.

"Pete, how are you doin'?" I asked.

"I'm ok. So, this is your cousin? He seems cool. I have a lot of comic books. Some are really old. He says he's into video games too. What are you guys doing today? Is your sister…. I mean the ghost home? I was in so much trouble for having that written on me in black paint. I didn't think it was ever gonna come off. I had to scrub really hard, my stomach almost bled. What are you guys doing today? Busy? Wanna hang out?" Pete rambled nervously

"I think Captain Dictator has a voice recorder. The next time I'm here, I'll have to bring it so I can record, you then play it over again, much slower." Brady said with a laugh.

"Calm down Pete, don't be nervous. We can't understand a word you just said." I encouraged.

"Can I hang out with you all? My mom and dad are both at work. I'm bored." Pete said, after taking a deep breath.

"Sure, the more the merrier." Brady insisted with enthusiasm.

"No, Pete. As scared as you were yesterday, you don't want to do what we are doing today. You should just go back home and be bored." I said, not wanting to drag Pete into the mess were we in.

"Please guys? I promise I won't be any trouble. I'll try not to talk too fast, or at all if you want." Pete begged.

"Whatever. Don't get all freaked out like yesterday, and we will be ok." I replied.

"Are you guys ready? We haven't got a lot of time, and it is getting away from us." Brady rushed.

"What is getting away from us?" Pete asked.

"Time. Come on. Let's do this and get it over with." Brady said, walking to the back yard.

"Do what?" Pete asked curiously.

"Just come on if you are going with us. It's a long story. Keep up, stay quiet, and don't freak out. Ok?" I barked, dreading the journey ahead.

We walked quietly through the back yard, crossed the fence in front of the barn, walked through the overgrown pasture, and stood at the tree line.

"And here we are. Which way Captain Catastrophe?" I asked

"I was hoping you would have an idea. After all, it is your land, your haunting, and your butt we are trying to save." Brady laughed.

"How about that way?" Pete suggested, pointing to the right.

"Why that way?" I asked.

"Because if we go left, we will end up in a field. If we go straight, we will walk straight through, and end up in the same field. If we go right, we will be in the middle of the woods." Pete informed.

"Works for me. How about you Brady?"

"Sure. We don't even know what we are looking for, or which way to go. So, yeah, I'm ok with it." Brady agreed, still looking a little too excited for this.

Standing at the tree line, I knew it was all downhill from here. I mean literally all downhill. The land was all drastically sloping earth, pausing ever so often to level out, then slope farther down. Running water in a creek bed echoed up to the top of the hill. A sound both peaceful, and aggravating at the same time, because it made you have to use the bathroom really, really bad. Reaching the creek bed, I looked back up the hill. Our barn roof was still visible just above the hill top. I knew at this moment, we were in for the long haul.

"Hey guys, hurry up!! Come check this out! I've never seen anything like it!! How did it get way up there?" Brady called after venturing ahead around a bend in the creek.

"That is insane!" I replied, as I caught up and saw what he was talking about.

"I hope it doesn't fall on us. That could kill someone!!" Pete yelled.

"How is it even staying there? Is it tied or something?" I asked, looking up in a tall tree at a small, old, fishing boat resting between two tree limbs.

"I don't see anything holding it other than the limbs. It is pretty wild." Brady marveled.

"How would it have gotten up there?" Pete chimed.

"If it was on the ground, and the tree started growing up from underneath" I was cut off by Brady.

"No way. If the tree were a sapling, there is no way the branches would have been strong enough to hold it. They would have slipped right off, and grown around it." Brady smirked.

"Yeah, I guess you are right. So, do you think someone carried it up there?" I asked with a laugh.

"Well, I doubt that happened. I guess we may never really know." Brady resolved.

"Maybe the wind from a tornado could have blown it up there." Pete theorized.

"You could be right. More than likely that's what happened. Oh well, let's see what else we can find." I replied, getting a little more relaxed and focusing on the adventure I had been hoping for all summer. Searching for the evil entity had left my mind completely.

"Shawn!! I know something you could do, an experiment of sorts!!" Brady said, sounding like he had just discovered the secret to winning the lotto.

"What kind of experiment?" I asked attentively.

"You should come down here and walk the creek from time to time, just to keep an eye on the erosion. Keep track of it, and see firsthand how much the creek changes over time." Brady suggested.

"Sounds a little boring. That could take years, decades or longer wont it? I guess I could though, it would be cool to see how much it changes in ten or twenty years." I replied, taking it into consideration.

"Yeah, I didn't think of that. I will do the same. Right now, we should be somewhere behind my house. I don't think I've been much farther than this." Pete added.

These woods were unlike the others I had been in. A thick leafy blanket was sprawled all over the woodland, smothering out any attempt of vegetation. Several other dry creeks were scattered about, twisting turning, and descending from the opposing hill sides. Tree tops were in full bloom, hiding the clear blue sky overhead. Sun light glittered here and there, through tiny openings between the stretching leaves.

"Just wondering, do either of you guys have a watch or phone? Anything at all that tells time?" I asked, hoping one of them did.

"I don't have anything." Brady mumbled.

"Me either. I could run to my house and see what time it is. …but I don't know for sure how to get there from here." Pete replied.

"I wonder how long it has been since we left my house?" I asked.

"I'd say only a few minutes. I doubt it's been very long at all. I'm sure we still have plenty of time. Why?" Brady responded, sounding pretty certain.

"I just don't want to be in more trouble than I already am. You really think it's only been a few minutes?" I asked, needing some assurance.

"Oh yeah. No way it's been over ten or fifteen minutes." Brady replied.

"That's good. So, we have like an hour and fifteen minutes before we have to be back right?" I asked again.

"Sounds about right." Brady agreed.

We continued along the side of the creek bed, walking in it, on either side, and across it from time to time. Truly amazing territory, but no fascinating discoveries had been made since the old fishing boat in the tree top.

Trudging onward, it seemed like we had been wondering aimlessly through the woods for a millennium. Only the sounds of woodland creatures could be heard. Squirrels running from here to there searching for food, could be heard rustling around, possibly even following us, curious about the strangers who are invading their homes.

A steady roar became evident off in the distance. Increasing with each step we took. No doubt, a waterfall. This time, I would not be too afraid to see it up close.

"You guys hear that?" I asked with a smile.

"Yeah what is it?" Pete asked.

"I'll race ya!" Brady said, looking at me excitedly.

We broke into a run, running faster than I probably ever have. Pete running behind us, struggling to keep up. Hills on either side of the creek became too steep to run on, so we jumped in the creek and pushed on. Pete fell when he leaped in, making the same horrid half splash, half splat sound that I normally make when falling. Brady and I chuckled as we kept running as fast as we could. For the first time since the move, I was actually enjoying myself, hanging out with motor mouth Pete from down the street, and my crazy cousin Brady.

By the time we arrived at the waterfall, we were soaking wet. While running in the creek, each step splashed water everywhere. The deeper the creek got, the harder we had to work to run, splashing the creek water high over our heads at times.

Brady and I stopped inches away from the edge, awestricken by the beauty of the land and the lake below. We were speechless as we looked over the massive waterfall. The pretty blue water far below us looked inviting, begging us to take a leap of faith and dive off into the cool water. If I knew how to swim, I would have done just that. This day, seemed to be getting better by the second.

10

Moments later, our admiration was interrupted by pitiful whimpers coming up from behind. Pete was injured pretty bad. Blood oozed from a gash in his leg and dripped down his shin. He leaned forward as he walked, holding his outer thigh as he hobbled toward us in the creek. Trying to be tough, the pain was more than he could bare, whimpering and crying through clenched teeth as he drew nearer.

"Oh man, are you ok? Looks like that is really painful." I blurted.

"Yeah dude. You might need to go get some stiches in that. It looks really deep." Brady added.

"I guess we should be heading back anyway. I don't know how long we've been gone, but I'm sure it's been too long." I advised.

"For sure." Brady said.

"How did you do that anyway Pete?" I asked.

"When I jumped off into the creek, I fell down. I hollered for you guys to stop, to come back, but you just kept running away. I wouldn't have done that to you all." Pete said pitifully.

"I didn't hear you. I swear I didn't. If I had, then I would've stopped and gone back." I replied sternly.

"I honestly didn't hear you either dude. I guess the water splashing was too loud." Brady replied.

I glanced all around us in the woods, finally spying a broken tree limb. It looked a little rotten, but would be good enough for Pete to use as a walking stick until we got back.

"Here buddy. This should help keep your weight off of that leg. Even though we are dumb and didn't realize what had happened, we are with you now, and will get you back home soon." I ensured.

"Yeah, sorry about running off and leaving you." Brady apologized.

"It's ok, I guess. As long as it doesn't happen again." Pete demanded.

"Hey Brady. I just remember the whole point in making this trip. What was your big plan anyway? So far, we haven't seen anything resembling anything, have we?" I inquired.

"Well, I really didn't have a plan. The idea was to simply take a walk in the woods. It's like in every single horror story or film, people end up somewhere they shouldn't be. They unknowingly wander into the monster's domain, then… well we all know how they end." Brady stammered.

"So basically, we are merely bait. Bait that might not survive for that matter. Like I said, I hate the idea of it." I grunted.

"Are we hunting more ghosts?" Pete asked.

"Something like that. The ghost in my house appeared to me and Brady last night. She said some form of evil dwelled out here in the woods, and if we could lure it back to my house, then she would take care of it. Kill it or something." I stated.

"I was kinda hoping things would have worked out better than they have. Your typical wrong place, wrong time scenario." Brady added.

"I'm glad things are working out just the way they are. I mean, we are out here in the middle of nowhere. What are the odds of us coming face to face with the evil spirit, and actually making it back home so she can kill it?" I asked doubtfully.

"Slim to none would be my guess. More so now that my leg is all hacked up. If I had known this is what you guys were doing, I would've gone back home and been happily bored by myself. The creepy ghost at your house was too much for me. I hope I never see another one. You two could've told me you were going on some suicide mission." Pete belted.

"Pete has a point. I really had no plans on how to make it back if we did find it, him, or whatever. I hope you're not mad." Brady agreed.

"I am just a little. Here we are, pretty much just sitting ducks, wondering around looking for God knows what. We have no kind of defense at all against this thing. I can't run fast. You can run faster than me…wait…was that it? Just run off and leave me behind to get eaten? Torn to shreds? Sliced up? All while you go running back to tell my parents 'oh no some monster ripped Shawn to pieces! By the way, can I have his stereo and crappy comic books?" I bellowed.

"What are you talking about? Of course not! I'm right here with you aren't I? Who would even want your crappy comics anyway?" Brady rebuked the idea.

"Guys, I hate to interrupt your feud. But where the heck are we at? I don't remember seeing any of this." Pete trembled.

"This is odd. There was only one creek on the way down here, wasn't there? I mean, there are three now, but these other two were not here before. Were they?" I asked, baffled by the sight sitting before us.

"Never mind that, where did these old army vehicles come from? Even if we had passed through here before, we would have noticed them." Brady added.

Standing before a trident style merger of three creeks, old rusted down military vehicles filled the broad area of land around the conjunction. Some on all four wheels, what was left of them anyway. Others were overturned completely, or on their sides. Gravel sized areas sprinkled on some of them, showed bits of green camouflage. Rust had successfully overtaken most of them. A couple looked as though they had caught fire and burned.

"How could we have missed this? It's just not possible. I don't remember any part of the creek being this wide open before. On our way down here, the hills stood close on either side. Not like this." I raved.

"I know it. Maybe we are getting close to what we are looking for. Think one of these old trucks or jeeps could, be it?" Brady said with a laugh.

"I doubt it. Which way do you think we should go to get back?" I asked.

"They all look the same. Each of the three creeks, look identical." Pete pointed out the obvious.

"The one on the left maybe?" I asked, confused about the direction.

"Think horror films. …I'm betting on the one in the middle." Brady sneered.

"Why the one in the middle? I'm thinking the one on the left. Simply because I don't think we would have come from the one in the middle. With it leading straight into this destruction, there is no way we could have missed it." I replied with uncertainty.

"Yeah, but that could be the same for the one on the right. I mean, the one on the right would seem the best bet. If we had walked down from that way, maybe we could have missed this war zone. Running, and rounding the bend here, could have caused us to overlook all of this destruction." Pete rationalized.

"God I'm so confused. Brady, why do you think the one in the middle, when it's obviously not right?" I demanded.

"For that reason alone, because it's not the obvious choice. Gotta think in terms of horror." Brady explained.

"Ok, so you think the one in the middle will get us back home. Not just back home, but back home safely?" I verified.

"I believe so. Yeah. Since it is without a doubt, not the way we came, I think it is. If Mr. Evil thingamajig has set this up to trick us, I think that is how. Making the obvious seem anything but." Brady added.

"I hope your right about this." I pleaded.

"I'm not going that way. I'm almost certain we walked the creek to the right, and that's the way I'm going." Pete barked stubbornly.

"No! Trust me you do not want to go that way. I really don't know why, but it is not the right way back." Brady exclaimed.

"Really? Just watch me hobble along." Pete barked again.

"No don't Pete. In a strange way, what Brady is saying does make sense. Besides, we are going to make sure you get back home. We aren't running off and leaving you, and you said you would not do that to us. We need to stick together, no matter which way we go." I suggested.

"Whatever. I'm going this way. When I get home, I'll tell your parents about you being lost in the woods, and where to come to find you two idiots." Pete grunted.

"Pete." I started.

"Shh, listen. …Do you hear that?" Brady whispered

"Hear what? All I hear is Pete stomping through the creek." I whispered back

"No, it's not Pete. Something is there. Behind us. Listen carefully, and you can hear it in the leaves. I can't see anything, but something is back there. I can hear it, and it feels like we are being watched." Brady replied quickly.

Brady and I turned, looking behind us. I didn't hear it at first, then something did start moving. It was on a hill to our left, beyond the trees and huge rocks, avoiding our sight, rustling in the leaves. Slow and careful steps were being taken to remain hidden, all the while, drawing in closer to us.

"HELLLPPPPP!!!" Pete yelled.

Turning quickly, it looked like Pete was sitting down in the creek bed.

"What happened? Did you fall again?" I asked

"NOOOOO! I'm SINKING!" Pete cried.

"I told him the one on the right wasn't the correct way. The creek, all the way down to the falls, had rock in the bottom. So why is he now sinking in mud?" Brady bellowed, aggravated that Pete had not heeded his warning.

"Fine, you told us so. Help me get him out!" I ordered.

Evidently, Brady's assumption was correct. Pete had only walked a short distance up the creek bed to the right, still holding tight to his walking stick. Being fairly long, he used the limb to keep his upper body from going under.

I ran up to the left side of Pete, stopping suddenly as the ground started to give way underneath my feet.

"Pete, can you hold on to the limb, and get it close enough for me to reach it?" I asked, hoping Brady and I could reach it and pull him out.

"I don't want to let go, but I can try." Pete answered, beginning to inch the tree limb over to me.

"That's it, slow and easy Pete." Brady encouraged, standing a few feet behind me and still watching behind us.

Pete moved his hands as far to the right of the limb as he could get. Not being able to reach the very end of it, he thrust it forcefully toward me, and quickly moved his left hand down to the very end to get it closer to me. The limb came straight at me, then suddenly bobbled in the air as Pete fell farther under the earth. I jumped high into the air, and farther over the mud to grab it as Pete's head disappeared.

"BRADY!!!!!!" I yelled grasping the limb in one hand, and reaching back for Brady with the other. When my feet hit the mud, it felt like there was nothing there. Feet, ankles, and calf muscles quickly slipped through the ground. My life flashed before my eyes. If this was it, if this were my time to go, I could say is life really hasn't been too bad. I've seen on tv that in quick sand, you should remain as still as possible to slow the sinking. I did just that. No movement. No talking. I didn't even breathe. I've never been in quick sand, but I was sinking at a steady pace in this muck. I hoped Pete could hold his breath for a long time. He was submerged in the gunk already. My end of the limb, barely visible now with my upper body slipping down into the mud pit.

My arm still reaching for Brady, he kneeled just outside of the quick mud, reaching for my hand, inching a little closer, a little closer….

"I can't reach you! Hang on I've got to go find something!" Brady panicked.

'Hang on to what? I'm hanging onto a limb now, and it's not doing me any good!' I think to myself. Mud now up to my neck, as I continued to remain calm, while sinking deeper into the cold thin mud. Teary eyed, I wasn't ready for this. Death had always been far from my mind, receiving little to no thought at all. Still, this wasn't how I wanted it all to end. I felt the mud creeping up my chin. I inhaled a deep breath, the deepest one I had ever taken, and held it before my face went under. Mud went up into my nostrils, seeped into my ears, my eyes closed pushing out the excessive water. Everything went dark………

11

Brady ran from one army vehicle to the next, scanning each inside and out, for rope or anything of potential use. The odds of finding anything remotely fitting that description were slim. Even if any rope or cable had been present, they would have been weathered far beyond use.

"God come on!! Help me out a little!!" Brady yelled in a rage. Searching the vehicles as fast as he could, only one remained, and time was running out. Rusty hinges screeched as he yanked the door open fully. Glancing around inside, there was nothing other than rotten seats, and insect infested floor boards.

"Come on! Think… What can I use?" Brady yelled again, clasping his face in both hands. His heart raced, adrenaline rushing through his body. Suddenly, he noticed a tall sapling growing by the mud trap. He climbed almost to the top of it, high enough for it to bend over, then moved farther to the tip top, forcing it closer to the mud. Shawn's finger tips slowly sunk down into the earth. Brady held on to the sapling for dear life, as the top of the tree came down fast, his feet crashing on solid earth.

"What?? What is this?? How has it dried up? Where the heck is the mud??? SHAAAAAAWNN!!!! PEEEETE!!!!!" Brady cried, releasing the sapling and clawing the hard ground, digging frantically. Brady hoped to find anything, a hand, Shawn's hair, or even the limb they were both holding to. Just one sign they were still there, would have been enough to keep going.

It would have been enough motivation to dig until they were out, and the three of them could continue their adventure. However, he found nothing. It was as though the mud pit had swallowed them whole, then dried hard as concrete.

Leaves rustling even closer now smacked Brady back to reality. Breathing heavily, he glared in the direction of the noise. Though he could not see anything, there was something there. Stalking its prey before moving in for the kill.

"Ok, Ok. Horror films. What have we got now? Two people dead…maybe not…sometimes they are taken, but are still alive... God, I hope that's the case. Three creeks, which way to go? Obviously not this way. Shawn thought the one on the left. I hope I'm right. I have to go with my gut on this one." Brady rambled quickly, wiping tears from his face.

With something slithering right toward him, through the vast amount of leaves on the ground, he got to his feet and ran. Not wanting to wait around and find out what it was that had been following them, he ran as fast as he could up the creek in the middle. Leaves being pushed side to side, possibly even being swooped up by someone's toes dragging behind him, increased steadily. It was the hunter, and he was the prey.

His muscles burned. His body ached. His heart pounded faster and faster, like a ticking time bomb. Energy draining vigorously with each step.

"I can't go on. I have to rest." Brady said faintly, crashing to the ground. His stalker seemed to cease in its mad dash for him as well.

The wind blew around him in a broad circle, creating small leafy tornados whizzing past. Brady's chest felt crushed, lungs on fire. Sweat sprouted up all over him, drenching his clothes, and rolling into his eyes. He panted, gasping for air as he lay on his back in this woodland.

"Hey you. Yeah you. Come on in, and get a nice cold glass of water." A deep, scruffy voice called to him.

"What?" Brady asked.

"Come on inside son. Nothing but fun times, cool air, and ice water in here." The voice insisted.

"Where are you?" Brady asked.

"I think I'm in front of you. I can't see you, but I can hear and smell you." The voice said.

"Are you blind?" Brady asked, getting to his feet and looking around. His eyes still burning from the sweat.

"Not at all. I see everything. Unfortunately, I cannot see through walls." The voice blurted.

Brady looked around wildly trying to pinpoint where the voice was coming from.

"Come on in… Braaaadyyyy. Your pals are in here with me. They are taking naps right now…I think so anyway. They must be worn out. No life left in them at all." The voice said, laughing a spine-chilling laugh.

"I don't believe you!! How do you know our names??" Brady demanded.

"I know everything Brady. NOW GET IN HERE!!!" The voice growled.

Startled, Brady put his back against the nearest tree, an old, hollow tree, standing roughly ten feet in the air. No limbs, just a tall, hollow post. The top was jagged, appearing severed from the rest by a lightning strike.

"I won't ask again." The voice whispered, almost in Brady's ear.

With hair standing on the back of his neck, Brady realized he had picked the wrong tree. Scared stiff, he hesitated.

'Should I make a run for it? Should I stand and try to fight? What usually works in the movies?' Brady thought to himself.

Long, thin, rootlike fingers, slipped around Brady's left ankle before he could finish his train of thought. A sudden yank sent him flying face first onto the ground. Looking back at his ankle, being pulled into an opening at the bottom of the hollow tree, he began kicking as hard as he could to free himself. Kicking, grabbing for anything that could give him some leverage. One violent kick struck the bottom of the tree, knocking a huge chuck of it inward.

"Come on Brady. It's so much fun in here! SO, STOP STRUGGLING!" The voice growled.

"Not today weirdo!" Brady blurted out, with adrenalin starting to pump through his veins again. Latching on to some tree roots, Brady kicked as hard as he could, and pulled with every ounce of strength that he had.

"Come on, you know ya wanna see your friends again!!! NOW LET GO!!!" The voice beckoned.

Brady looked to his feet, wanting to put a face with the voice. A red glow filled the inside of the hollow tree, as if fire were dancing around inside. He took a deep breath, kicked, and pulled until the monster's grip slipped off of his ankle. He ran, he ran as though his life depended on it. Thunder clouds flooded into the sky, blotting out what sunlight peaked through the leafy tree tops. Wind gusts erupted behind him, stopping short of his heels, hesitating, then erupting again, stirring fallen leaves and plucking lively ones from branches.

Hurrying up the creek, he could see the familiar sight of the fishing boat in the tree top, during lightning flashes. A little farther, he turned hard left, and raced up the sloping hill toward Shawn's house.

"God help me!! God help me!!" Brady chanted. His legs feeling like jelly, and his adrenaline fading fast.

Sunlight remained, pouring down on Shawn's house, barn and field. Storm clouds rampaged right behind Brady, as he raced as much as he could on spaghetti noodle legs. Wind swooped at his feet, or maybe it was the monster, trying angrily to get Brady in his clutches once again.

Nearing the gate, Brady leaped into the air, landing on it midway, and bounced over the top. He fell on his back, as the storm clouds swarmed in overhead.

"Susan!!! Susan!!! He's here!!!" Brady yelled to the ghost.

Lightning struck all around Brady, as winds of a hurricane crashed against the fence and the barn. The sky above the field was blackened by dust, dirt, and debris being carried in the winds.

"SUSAN!!!! PLEASE!!!!" Brady begged.

"Now I've got you. Too tired to run, are you?" The voice spoke cheerfully.

"Susan, help me. Help Shawn and Pete!" Brady cried.

Leaves, sticks, stones, and other debris flew through the air, attacking Brady as he lay on the ground. Exhausted, he got back on his feet to make one final run for the house. As he turned his back to the devastating storm, she was there. Clumsily, along with a gust of wind, he staggered and fell through the ghost.

"You have no one. Not now, nor ever again." Susan spoke to the storm peacefully.

"You, witch! I've already took your life, now I'll devour what is left!!!" The voice hissed, being carried through the wind.

The storm calmed a great deal. Black clouds still filled the sky. 'the calm before the storm' Brady thought to himself. Looking to Susan, her eyes were locked on something in the field. Wind blew steadily in a circular motion, bobbing up and down just above the ground. When it finally hit the ground, the weak tornado died. There in the field, was a bald man. His eyes were dark, almost black, though not as black Susan's were. He stood, glaring at Susan for a few moments.

Brady, frozen stiff, overwhelmed with fear, could not look away. Clothed in green camouflage, the man started walking toward Susan. His hands rolled into tight fists, white knuckles blaring through the darkness. The bald man, nearing Susan, began laughing and shaking his head.

"You should run along now Missy. You never stood a chance before, so you should know better than to stand, or float against me now!!" the man growled.

"Your time here is over. You have to answer for what you have been doing in your past life, as well as this one you have made for yourself. I have been sent here to bring you to justice, one way or another." Susan stated peacefully.

"Sent here by who?" the man demanded.

"You know who sent me. He has a message for you. Your evil doings will no longer be tolerated. You should have stayed where you were, before returning here." Susan bellowed.

The bald man laughed his evil laugh, smacked himself in the head, and turned in retreat. After only a few steps, he turned to face Susan once more.

"Yeah Missy, we will just see about THAT!!" The man growled. The wind picked up speed as the man laughed, faster and faster, until another, stronger tornado plummeted to the ground where he was standing.

Brady watched as trees were pulled up by their roots in the woods, and began swirling through the air.

Winds thrashed around in the field and wooded area at massive speeds. The sky blackened again. Trees, possibly even the old fishing boat, army vehicles, and other debris, was thrust about with vicious force. The roar of the wind, and thunder booming, was deafening.

"Susan!! I hope you had a plan for this!! This is what you wanted isn't it?" Brady yelled to her.

Susan turned to look at him. The old decayed corpse of a young woman looked him in the eye, and gave a slight wink from a dark empty socket. Her arms reached up and out on either side, palms facing the brutal storm. She seemed to hold this hurricane at bay, not allowing the raging storm to pass beyond the fence. Her hair and dress rippled gently, as if it were only a cool breeze on a hot summer day. Lightning struck the ground, blowing huge chunks of dirt up in Brady's face. He quickly inched further back behind Susan.

Large trees were hurled toward Susan. With telekinetic like abilities, she would throw them back into the storm. An intense assault of trees, the fishing boat, lightning bolts, and old army vehicles, thrust toward her at great speeds. Growing more intense, the storm raged on and on, for what felt like hours. Susan, absorbed all of the punishment it could dish out. A fierce gust of wind blew, forcing the levitating ghost to float backward, away from the fence. Her rotten midnight blue dress coming apart, along with what flesh had been intact on her maggot infested body.

Tears began flowing up toward Brady's hair line, as the wind blew harder and harder. He began doubting her ability to be successful in her revenge with this puppet master, as she called it. His eyes squinted, just trying to keep visual on what was happening. Suddenly, a large army truck was slung from the dark sky.

"Susan!" Brady yelled as the truck flew toward him. One of the front rusty wheels stopped firmly against his nose. Susan motioned with one of her hands, sending it flying back into the black mass, as Brady let out a sigh of relief.

Susan shoved forward, going higher in the air, arms out stretched, with the storm's focus being entirely on her now. It made Brady think of kids challenging each other with a line in the dirt, daring each other to cross it. A six-rung, barbed wire fence, playing the part of the line between the two. An endless assault of lightning bolts, relentlessly stabbed at Susan.

With the noise surpassing deafening levels, Brady plugged his ears with his fingers. Susan was practically inhaling most of what this storm had to offer, but some of what it carried was getting past her. Random trash continued pelting Brady in the face, his eyes seeming to be the target.

Brady watched, reaching the conclusion that Susan was involved in a losing battle. Retreating briefly, the storm resumed its havoc on Susan, with all of the fury it could produce. Meaning well, the withered ghost flew to pieces and was carried away into the wind.

"What??? Susan!!!! Susan!!!!!" Brady cried. The storms wind, slowed down suddenly, making weird puffs, and the sound of someone coughing. Trees fell from the sky, becoming lodged in the ground inverted, along with the fishing boat, abandoned army vehicles and other objects that had been swept up into the air. Brady ran, zig zagging through the yard to avoid being crushed by something falling from the sky.

Storm clouds flickered, as brief flashes of lightning quivered behind them. A flash occurred, but did not go away. It seemed to grow brighter from a dull glow. Brady covered his eyes when it grew to a blinding degree. Bursting through the sky, the light was gone. Brady looked up to the storm clouds. To his surprise, they were rapidly dissipating. Rain plummeted to the ground like being dumped from a pail.

"That's it. It's all over now. No more ghost lady, no more Shawn or Pete." Brady said, weeping in between the battered barn, boards, and roofing, falling off of it, and the undamaged house. "What am I going to tell Shawn's parents? What are they going to tell Pete's parents?"

"You won't be telling them anything, you little brat!!" The man said, holding his side and staggering toward Brady. The man appeared beaten to a point beyond that of survival, bleeding severely from a dozen wounds.

"Please, what do you want? Just leave me alone!!" Brady begged.

"Just your soul! It's all fun and games, until you lose that!!! I'm going to swallow yours!!" The man said, licking his lips, closing in on Brady.

"I told you, I'm taking you back one way or another!!" Susan grunted from the sky. Her boney hand motioned as if to grasp him by the throat, then yanked him up into the air.

<u>12</u>

Dazed, confused, waiting, and hoping it was finally over. Brady constantly looked over his shoulder. He waited cautiously, searching all around the surrounding area for over an hour, expecting the strange man to reappear, and to reach out and drag him back to the hollow tree at any second. Eventually, Brady realized it was just that, finally over.

Getting his nerve up to break this kind of news to the parents of the boys, wasn't easy. If only he could have been torn apart and whisked away in the storm like Susan, he would have been happy. With any luck, he imagined being put in a mental hospital, declared mentally unstable, and locked up in a padded room. A thought of jail or prison was more than Brady could handle just now. However, finding himself locked away in either place wouldn't stop people from calling him a murderer, and gossiping about how he killed his cousin and neighbor. They would talk about how cruel Brady must be to do such a thing, and leave no trace of evidence that it even occurred.

"I really wanna run away. Why did I ever want to do this to begin with? Shawn's parents are going to kill me." Brady mumbled to himself.

Eyes full of tears, and sobbing uncontrollably, Brady began his walk of disgrace. Being broken at the thought of being the messenger of the worst news possible. Head hanging low, leaving a trail of tears, he stomped up to the front door of Shawn's house.

~ 138 ~

"Cheryl. Dan., I need help. Shawn and Pete need help!!" Brady shouted into an empty house. His sobbing was far from reaching its end, as he took a seat at the kitchen table. His elbows were planted firmly on the placemat, and his hands were holding his forehead as tears splattered on the table one after another. He opened his eyes and looked around the kitchen, then the hall. Getting up to enjoy one last glass of strawberry soda, before he met his doom, he found a note on the refrigerator door:

Shawn & Brady,

We have gone to town. Be back soon. Stay out of trouble while we are gone.

Love,

Mom

"Well, looks like my death sentence has been postponed a little longer." Brady mumbled.

With a tall glass of strawberry soda in hand, Brady walked into Shawn's bedroom and sat on the edge of the bed. He looked around at Shawn's belongings. A large box sitting on the dresser marked "Comics" made Brady's stomach roll. The half-assembled stereo on the night stand reopened the flood gates.

"I'm sorry Shawn! I really am. I tried to save you, but I couldn't!!" Brady shouted, looking up to the ceiling and bawling his eyes out.

"Brady? Where are you?" Shawn asked, his voice muffled and distant.

"Oh great. Now you are going to torment me from the great beyond. Aren't you?" Brady sobbed.

"I don't know. I guess if I am dead. Am I dead? I don't feel dead. I mean, I feel like a statue with all of this mud on me." Shawn responded, his voice muffled and distant.

"I hate being dead because my stupid leg still hurts! I didn't think dead people could feel any pain!" Pete said angrily, his voice muffled and distant also.

"Where are you guys? Make some noise. I can barely hear you two. Bang on something or…I don't know, just anything. Do something!" Brady yelled.

"I think I've found something. Can you hear this?" Shawn asked, banging on something, his voice was still muffled and distant.

"Ok, Yes. Yeah. Yes! I hear a…a…. a… thumping sound. Now I just have to figure out where you guys are!" Brady cheered.

He followed the thumping sound to the hallway. It was clearly coming from underneath the floor. He hurried to the basement, but no sign of Shawn or Pete.

Listening intently, he realized they were on the other side of the wall, somewhere underneath Shawn's parents' room. Brady raced upstairs, and into their bedroom.

"Ok, Shawn, you all are under the floor of your parents' bedroom. Can you all see anything? Any light, or a door?" Brady yelled.

"No, it's pitch black down here. How the heck did we even end up in here??" Shawn inquired.

"I don't care how. I just want out so I can take a long shower." Pete grumbled.

"Alright, alright. I'm working on it." Brady yelled.

'Think, think, how do I get them out?' Brady thought to himself. Searching for a door or something, loose floor board perhaps, he slung the closet door open and rummaged through the hanging clothes. Nothing. He checked the walls, feeling of them carefully for a hidden doorway. No luck. He sat down on the bed.

"Guys what do I do? How do I get you all out? I'm running out of ideas here." Brady pleaded.

"I'm running out of patience myself. It smells like Susan in here!" Shawn bellowed.

"Thump on something again so I can get an idea of exactly where you all are." Brady requested.

As the next thump happened, Brady glimpsed the carpet lifting from under the bed. Jumping to his feet, he slid the bed over toward the door. There, on the carpet, were faint lines rectangular in shape. Grabbing two fists full of carpet, he stripped it back away from the wall uncovering a trap door. It was flawless in design, appearing one with the rest of the floor. The edges sat higher than the rest by only a fraction of an inch, and a small thumb hole at one corner for opening.

Lifting the door, he saw Shawn and Pete. The two were covered in dried mud, while Shawn held a skull in his hand, using it to make the thumping noise.

"Man, I bet that is going to be some bad karma for you." Brady said sternly.

"Gross!!!" Shawn yelled flinging the skull away from him.

"Honestly, I would hug you guys if you two weren't covered in mud." Brady stated, wiping tears from his eyes.

"Same to you if your face wasn't all scratched up, bloody, and covered in knots." Pete stammered.

"What happened to you guys? I was trying to save you, then the ground just dried up. I tried to dig you out, but you were not there." Brady asked.

"I don't know. One minute we were sinking, then next we were falling into a cave. We couldn't see anything, just had to feel our way around in some cave or tunnel. We didn't even know where we were. We screamed and hollered until our throats hurt, then we gave up until you started bawling like a little baby." Shawn giggled.

"Yeah, you are a little bit of a cry baby." Pete added.

"Pete, where is your shirt??" Brady asked.

"I thought it would help, when we were stuck in the mud. I wrapped it around the tree limb. It could have clogged up the opening to the cave I guess." Pete mumbled.

Brady and I both chuckled at Pete.

"So, what happened to you? I'm guessing you had a fun trip back. Did Susan hold up her end of the bargain?" I asked. Pete and I listened to Brady's tale about the sudden crazy storm, and Susan getting blown to bits, followed by the sudden calm, and the weird bald man.

When mom and dad got back home, they were worried to death after they saw the destruction in our back yard and field. However, as with most parents, the second they saw their bedroom torn apart, and a ton of mud everywhere, the worry dissolved in an instant, and their tempers rocketed beyond furious. However, they actually listened to our story and seemed to believe it, for a change.

They called the authorities after looking at the remains of Susan down in the cellar, and had them removed. Sherriff Tom said that Susan had been listed as a missing person, an unsolved mystery running a course of longer than two decades. Sherriff Tom went on to tell us that a lot of people suspected her parents (Lloyd and Marge) of killing her and hiding the body, but no one could prove it. That was until now.

Lloyd and Marge, how they lived with themselves I'll never know. Even with the evil in the woods acting as puppeteer for them, I'm sure they still would have known what they were doing. If not during the act itself, then after the fact when they tossed her lifeless body down into the cellar. Keeping track of that in the newspapers, it seemed Lloyd and Marge were now residing in a mental asylum a few counties away.

This summer started out pretty rough, but with the ghost gone, and getting to know the calm Pete from down the street, it could be my most memorable summer ever. Our house is pretty nice too, aside from the dungeon, all of the blood red paint in my room, the creepy antique mirror, spooky upstairs, and the fact that I found skeletal remains of a girl I never knew in a cellar that we didn't know we had. The best part was, I had an adventure. One that exceeded my wildest dreams, and I still have over two months to perfect my first day of school tale. …On second thought, maybe it would be better for Halloween…. Nah, I don't think I could wait that long.

MY HAUNTED SCHOOL YEAR

Excerpt

1

Katherine left her meeting feeling even more disgusted than she had the first day of school last year. Each passing year the state's expectations grew slightly more unattainable than the last. Her feet already throbbing and aching as she hurried along to her classroom. The long years, now behind her, since she became a teacher, had taken their toll on her. 'What a sad way to start not just another day, but a brand-new school year. The bar was set high, so high for this year that the moral among fellow teachers was at an all-time low.' She thought to herself.

A time when her feet did not hurt, when the smooth floors of the school felt as such instead of fiery hot coals, was a time she could no longer remember. Summer breaks used to help revive not only her sore and aching extremities, but her devotion for this career as well. Eligibility for retirement was approaching within the new few years, if only she can hang on that much longer.

Turning down the pale blue hall of which her classroom sat midway, the commotion in the air let her know her new students for the year were wild. Evidently, the teacher who had been watching her class had apparently jumped ship. Picking up the pace, blood pressure rising, and her 1960's style glasses bouncing on her nose, she stepped inside and slammed the door.

"Sit down and be quiet this instant!!" -Katherine yelled, giving the marker board a loud whack with a yard stick as ancient as she was. "Now that I have your full attention, this type of behavior will not be tolerated in my classroom! You boys in the back, get down off of those desks! They were not made for standing and jumping on!! Rule number one for each and every one of you, respect me, my classroom, our learning materials, and I will respect you!! If not, if there is a breach at any level of that rule, you will find yourself in a world of trouble!!"

Her new students, terrified at this senile old lady, were frozen stiff. Only seconds before she walked in, they had been jumping around like a bunch of extra hyper monkeys. A couple good kids were being just that, sitting at their desks and waiting on their new teacher. Yet, the pain building in her feet and aching old bones needed some type of ventilation. Her angry outburst helped ease some of her frustration, and showed the students she had zero tolerance for their shenanigans.

Perched on her stool, behind a podium like an old buzzard, roll call began. Gradually making her way down the list of all twenty-five new students, and finding two of them were absent. Absent, on the first day of school.

"These two must be a couple of real goof balls, laying out on the very first day of school. Their parents letting them play hooky really said a lot about them as well. What kind of influence are they actually getting at home? Setting an example such as this." She thought.

I could hear my new teacher's loud and obnoxious voice echoing down the halls. A single voice all but comparable to nails on a chalk board. I was in a rush, walking the briskest walk imaginable, to get to class before the tardy bell rang. Each second had to count in my race to beat time.

This day had started out great for me. I couldn't sleep at all last night, laid awake in bed, going over and over what I would tell my classmates about my summer…only fluffed a very small amount by the way. I was actually up, out of bed, showered and sitting in the living room waiting, by the time mom had woken up and started breakfast.

I knew some of my fellow classmates accompanying me on the bus ride. None that I would really call friends, and only one or two that I socialize with just to be polite on occasion. Everything seemed just right, all factors for a great first day of the school year were present. Then, our bus ride got derailed, all of a sudden, when the driver was turning around in one kid's driveway. The driver managed to overshoot the driveway, and the bus sunk deep into the soft ground in the kids' yard. The driver was in denial about the current situation. Shifting the bus from reverse to drive, back and forth for several minutes.

"Must be the transmission going out. I thought it had been acting weird, and they were supposed to fix it over the summer!!" The driver grunted.

After he exited the bus to check the transmission fluid, me and a few other guys followed behind him.

"Hey, I think I found your problem back here. Is it supposed to look like this? I'm not a mechanic or anything so I don't know." I asked. Pete and the others burst out laughing.

"Look like what?" The driver demanded, walking toward the rear of the bus.

"The rear wheels are gone. I think they are either sitting somewhere deep down in the ground here, or maybe they have fallen off." Pete joked.

"Yeah Rusty, I can't even see the bumper back here anymore. I guess we lost it too, and half of the rear exit door." Luke said. We laughed looking at the back half of the bus buried deep down in the kids' yard.

"What are you all doin off the bus anyway? Get back on there. You aren't allowed to be off unless you are getting off the bus at school, or at home. So back on there with ya's." Bus Driver Rusty demanded, attempting to sound upset while embarrassment shone through.

Not pressing our luck, we got back on and took our seats. Then we waited, and waited, and waited some more, all the while waiting for Rusty to get up enough nerve to call the Director of Transportation, and report the incident. It was another hour long wait for an additional bus to show up with log chains, and pull our bus out of the little kids' yard.

With the bus finally moving again, Rusty continued to stop at every house on his route, and wait excessively for kids that never showed up. My guess was that their parents assumed they had missed the bus, and had taken them to school. Rusty was reluctant to believe that could have happened, thus putting our arrival time dangerously late.

My school absolutely loved bells for some reason or other. In the mornings, we had one that rang signaling the bus to let students exit, another one about fifteen minutes later meaning it was time to finish breakfast, and hurry on to first period, one five minutes later saying you should be in class and in your seat at this time (if you're not, you should be), and the last one occurring two minutes later meaning you were tardy if not already in your seat. While standing in line to exit the bus, I clearly heard the bell signaling the beginning of class, ring.

Fighting my way through the crowded halls, full of students hurrying on to whatever class they needed to be in, was time consuming. But here I was, speed walking down an empty hall toward Ms. Katherine's class, with no time to spare. Her door was almost arm's length away, when I felt a sudden, vaguely familiar slap across the back of my head.

"Was that really necessary Jon?" I blurted, immediately being slammed into the lockers. His big hands clutching my head like it was a basketball, holding me firmly against the locker, with my right cheek smashed against it.

"Shawn, I know all about you and your little story, you are just dying to tell to our classmates. I hate to burst your bubble, but it wasn't all you! The only thing you did was get lost in a cave, Brady did all of the real work. Not to mention, I have a pretty good story of my own that will make yours look like a baby's cartoon! In fact, mine is so good, you won't even have a chance to tell yours!!" Jon barked.

"Really? How do you know about all of that anyway?" I asked.

"I know because he told me everything." Jon replied.

"Who told you what??" I asked, becoming more upset.

"The Devil! He told me to tell you, he's coming for you, and there's nothing you can do to stop him." Jon snarled, releasing his grip from my head and neck, then running into his classroom.

Finally getting a glimpse of him as he ran into a classroom, he wasn't clothed as he normally was. Usually he wore nice, expensive brand name clothes, the kind I only wish I owned. This morning, he had on a dirty white T-shirt, with a big tire tread pattern going from the bottom left side, up to the top right. It must have been some kind of Motocross, or four-wheeling kind of shirt. His jeans looked like they had not seen a decent washing machine since a few months either. They were stained, dirty, and torn. His attire was the exact opposite of his usual flawless, pressed, and squeaky-clean type.

"What kind of crap was he trying to pull now? Brady wouldn't have said anything to him. Must have been Mike or Pete…Maybe Jon just read it in the news, and didn't even know what happened over the summer." I mumbled, walking into class and interrupting Ms. Katherines train of thought.

"Child, if this is going to be an everyday occurrence, you being tardy, then maybe you should go to the counselor's office, and get switched out of my class." Katherine said hatefully.

"No mam, it won't be. My bus broke down on the way here, and it caused me to be late. Look out the window and you might actually see my bus leaving, number 1999." I pleaded.

She looked at me strangely, as though I were only playing some weird joke on her, and the moment her back was turned, I would pelt her with spit wads or something.

"Take a seat." She said coldly, glaring at me over the top of her glasses.

The first empty chair I saw was in the back of the room, in the middle row. I walked to it and sat down as fast as I could.

"Are you Jon, or Shawn?" She asked in the same cold tone.

"Shawn, ma'am." I replied.

"Hey Mike, I thought you said Jon was staying back last year?" I whispered to Mike, who was sitting in the row beside of me.

"That was the word, but didn't you hear what happened?" Mike replied, with a puzzled look on his face.

"Hear what? He just slammed me into a locker right before I walked in, then he ran into the classroom across the hall." I replied

"Ok class, listen up, and stop…" Ms. Katherine started, cut off by the intercom.

"We have tragic news this morning. Some of you may know already, some might not. There was a tragic event that occurred over the summer to one of our own." Principal Bennet Pingson announced, his voice quivering as he spoke. "A dear fellow classmate, Jon Pingson, had his life cut short over the summer. Any of you that were close to him, if you need to talk, or if you need anything at all, feel free to come and see me, or counselor Jenna."

Jon. Dead. He just shoved me, face first, into the lockers. Unless…how nice is it that I now have another ghost, tormenting me? I thought, well, I hoped that it would be over with for good with Susan gone. So much for wishful thinking.

"Well, I think that just about sums it up. We have decided that today, we are not going to get things started as we normally would. You all may talk quietly amongst yourselves if you wish. Though, keep in mind if the volume starts getting out of hand, I will proceed as if it is simply any other school day. If any of you would like to say something about your classmate to the rest of the class, you may do so, but please maintain an orderly fashion taking turns, and do not try to speak over another student. If someone has something to say that could be misinterpreted as being disrespectful, please keep it to yourself." Ms. Katherine instructed.

Ms. Katherine turned her podium over to the class, and sat down behind her large desk in the corner.

The smart kids, and athletic kids were the first to stand before the rest of us, and say a few words in remembrance. I only knew one aspect of Jon; therefore, my remorse was almost nonexistent. Yet, the more they talked about the "Jon" they knew, I soon realized he might have actually been a decent person. My heart sank down into my stomach as my sympathy for those that knew him better than I, grew. It made me nauseous in a way. They all spoke as though he were nothing less than a saint. Why couldn't I have met that guy? Why did I have to meet the annoying bully instead?

"Are you ok man? I thought you knew about it. Would you like to say a few words?" Mike asked nervously.

"Of course not. I don't even know what I would say anyway. Oh, yeah, he was great. He bullied me all year in fourth grade, then (his ghost apparently), shoved me into a locker just this very morning. I think not. I will just listen to everyone else." I replied sarcastically.

"Seriously? I thought you might have been making it up." Mike stammered.

"Why would I make that up? What happened to him anyway?" I asked.

"I don't know. I just…never mind. I heard that he went to the building supply store with his dad one day over the summer. While they were there, he threw a fit wanting a new bike, his dad told him no, then he just got on one, and started riding it all through the store. I heard in the end, he was screaming and crying. They said his hands and feet were wrapped with some industrial strength tape as he sped out of the store, and right in front of a big diesel truck." Mike reported.

"His hands and feet were taped? Like someone or something forced him to do it? Why didn't he just hit the brakes, or ride around through the store until he found his dad?" I asked, puzzled by the intel.

"Yeah, pretty much. I heard there was a malfunction with the bike, that he was pedaling backwards-freely- trying to get it to stop, when he raced out of the store on it." Mike added.

"I don't remember seeing anything about it in the newspaper over the summer. I will have to look back through them when I get home. A different issue was going on that I was keeping track of, so I got a pretty good collection going on in my room." I mumbled.

"I don't know if it was in the newspaper or not because I never read them. I heard about it on the radio the day after it happened." Mike clarified.

"I guess that does explain the tire track on his shirt when he finally let go of me, and ran into the class across the hall." I blurted.................................